Five Nights at Freddy's™

FAZBEAR FRIGHTS #5

BUNNY CALL

Five Nights at Freddy's™

FAZBEAR FRIGHTS #5

BUNNY CALL

SCOTT CAWTHON
ELLEY COOPER
ANDREA WAGGENER

Scholastic Inc.

Copyright © 2020 by Scott Cawthon. All rights reserved.

Photo of TV static: © Klikk/Dreamstime

Library of Congress Cataloging-in-Publication Data available

ISBN 978-1-338-57604-7
2 2020

Printed in the U.S.A.   23

First printing 2020 • Book design by Betsy Peterschmidt

TABLE OF CONTENTS

The sun erupted from behind low-hanging gray clouds and nearly blinded Bob. He squinted, glowered, and flipped down the visor as he slowed to maneuver his anemic minivan around the millionth sharp curve on this seemingly endless winding road carving its way through thickly forested mountains.

That's . . . just . . . great, Bob thought.

The only thing he'd been looking forward to about this trip was the predicted rainy weather. His family was "bummed" about it, but he was secretly gleeful. Rain meant the flurry of activities would be canceled and he'd be left in peace to do a little fishing, take naps, and read a book.

"Honey, look at that!" Bob's wife, Wanda, sang out. "Sun!"

"Oh, is that what that is?"

She playfully smacked his shoulder.

"Hand me my sunglasses," Bob said.

Bob took his eyes from the road for a couple seconds and watched Wanda lean forward to dig the sunglasses out of the glove box. He admired her shiny auburn curls and the soft contours of her profile. Wanda was petite, pale, and freckled, with small features. Even after twelve years of marriage and three kids, she was still the pretty, perky cheerleader he'd fallen for when they were seniors in high school. The only noticeable difference was her clothes, having traded her pom-poms and pleated skirts for the latest fashion. Today, she was wearing high-waist short black shorts and a netted lavender top over a black tank. The top fell off one shoulder. It looked great.

Eyes back on the road, Bob put on his sunglasses. Then he took a couple seconds to check himself out in the rearview mirror. A couple seconds was all it took to confirm that he *didn't* look like the jock he'd been in high school

Gone were the long thick black hair, the sharp jawline, the mischievous dark brown eyes, and the wide, carefree grin. In their place were thinning, graying short hair, soft jowls, tired eyes, and lips clamped into a downward curve. Most of his muscles had gone wherever too much of his hair had gone. He didn't have enough time to work out . . . and it showed.

Bob quickly shifted his attention to the drive. He pulled the minivan into the right lane as the road starting climbing upward, and the two lanes turned into three, creating a passing lane. Two sporty sedans pulled out from behind Bob to zip right by.

Bob sighed. "I miss my MG."

Wanda glanced at him but wouldn't take the bait. She never did. She'd talked him into selling his beloved MG when they had their second child. He'd regretted it ever since. He missed everything about that car, even its smell— the distinct motor oil/leather seat smell that always made him feel manly . . . and young.

Bob shook his head and tried not to inhale the scents of the minivan: peanut butter, dirty socks, and grape juice.

"Guess what, everyone?" Wanda called out.

"What?" the kids chorused.

"They've changed the forecast!" Wanda did a little happy dance in her seat as she looked at her phone's screen.

Bob was surprised the phone still had service. It felt like they were thousands of miles from civilization.

"Instead of eighty percent chance of steady rain," Wanda

said, "it now says twenty percent. We're going to have sun!"

"Happy sun, smiling sun, sun come out to play," Bob's three-year-old daughter, Cindy, began singing off-key.

"Bright sun, friendly sun, it's a beautiful day," Wanda joined in with Cindy.

Cindy giggled and started in on the grating melody again. Her curly auburn pigtails bounced as she bopped through the song. What Cindy lacked in singing talent she made up for in cuteness and enthusiasm. Freckles and a happy grin won over everyone who met her.

"Come on, let's all sing!" Wanda called out.

Seven-year-old Aaron sat next to Cindy, in the car seat he was excited to be growing out of soon. He shared his sister's freckles and auburn hair as well as her energy, and predictably, joined in the singing. Tyler, ten, lanky and dark with broad shoulders that telegraphed the athletic build he'd have soon, lounged in his own space in the third row of seats. Tyler liked to set himself apart because he was the oldest, but he was still young enough to want to be included in family "fun." He still loved game night, movie night, Sunday picnics, and sing-alongs. Now he did his part by providing a beatbox backup.

"Happy sun, smiling sun, sun come out to play," Bob's family sang.

"Come on, Bob," Wanda cajoled, "sing!"

Bob grunted, then ground his teeth while his family went through the two lines at least half a dozen times. *Give me some classic rock and I'd belt out with the best of them,* Bob thought. But he wasn't going to sing about the stinking sun.

Bob kept his lips pressed together and his eyes on the road, where the still-wet pavement was glistening in the newly shining sun. The double yellow line was a tether pulling the minivan inexorably toward its destination. Bob might be driving, but he had no control. Not really.

When was the last time he'd had control? Before Tyler was born? When he and Wanda married? Before they met? Since he was born? Was control an illusion?

Finally the song wound down, and Aaron asked the age-old question, "Are we there yet?"

"Are we there yet? Are we there yet?" Cindy parroted.

"How much farther? Are we there yet?" Wanda asked Bob.

"Not you, too," Bob said with a sigh.

Wanda laughed. She looked at the map she had unfolded, and answered her own question. "Twenty-seven more miles," she said.

Bob found it endearing how Wanda insisted map-reading was more fun than using a GPS. It was one of the many quirks he loved about her. Making up songs—like the dumb sun song—was one of the many quirks he *wasn't* so crazy about. Harping continually on family togetherness was one of the quirks he truly hated.

When Tyler had been young, it wasn't so bad. Taking his son on fishing trips and to ball games was no trouble at all. Even the hikes Wanda had planned were fun. When Aaron was born, the family activities had gotten more complicated, but they had still been doable. Adding Cindy to the mix had raised the chaos factor tenfold. Cindy wasn't a brat or anything; she was actually a very sweet child. But her energy level was through the roof, and for some reason, all that did was amp up the boys. Lately, it seemed like Bob never got any peace or quiet, even at night. He could be sure that one or more of his kids would end up diving into bed with Wanda and him at some point, every night, without fail.

Where Bob used to have time to himself, now his time belonged to everyone *except* him. His work took a slice. His kids took a slice. Wanda took a slice. He never used to begrudge the time Wanda took, but that was because she wanted his time for fun things. Now all she wanted was for him to put on one of his many "family-man" hats: coach, teacher, playmate, cook, handyman, driver, shopper, janitor, money earner.

A couple months before, Wanda's best friend had told Wanda about Camp Etenia. "*Etenia* is a Native American name that means 'rich,'" Wanda read from the nearly magazine-thick brochure describing the place. "'We named our family-inclusive camp Etenia because a man who has family is indeed rich,'" she kept reading. "Isn't that beautiful, Bob?"

"Mm," he'd said absently.

Bob had thought Wanda was just reading about the place the same way she read about Greenland and Norway and Albania. Wanda wanted to travel, and she loved to research destinations. But it turned out Wanda was serious about Camp Etenia.

"Why don't we just send the kids to camp, and we can stay home and hang out in the hammock?" Bob asked when Wanda kept talking about it. He grabbed her and nuzzled her neck. "Just the two of us."

Wanda wasn't buying it. Neither did she approve of his idea that they go to a nice hotel and plop the kids by the pool so they could have time alone together. He finally pulled out all the stops and suggested a high-priced resort that promised to entertain the kids while the parents lounged under big umbrellas on white sandy beaches. Bob wanted to *relax*. Wanda wanted something else.

So here he was . . . on his way to Camp Etenia.

Bob glanced in his rearview mirror to find out why it was suddenly so noisy in the minivan. Now all three of his kids were engaged in some elaborate hand-clapping game.

Wanda leaned toward Bob. "Zoie and I used to love camp when we were little girls," she told him for the tenth time. "The only downside was that we had to be away from Momma and Daddy. Isn't it awesome we don't have to put the kids through that? We'll all be together for a full week!"

"Awesome."

If Wanda noticed his sarcasm, she ignored it.

A deer ran across the road in front of the minivan, and Bob hit the brakes. Thankfully, the minivan hadn't been going very fast. It couldn't. It had no pick-me-up for steep grades, especially at high altitudes. Even though he easily missed the deer, Bob felt his blood pressure go up.

"Can you keep it down?!" Bob bellowed at his kids. "I'm trying to drive up here."

Momentary silence.

"Do you think there are fairies in there, Daddy?" Cindy asked him. She was staring out the side window at the dense forest crowding the side of the road.

"Why not?" Bob said.

Wanda had told him over and over that Cindy was extra-sensitive. He could never "burst her bubble." If she wanted to believe there were fairies, it was his job to go along with it.

Wanda changed the subject. "So what are we going to do when we get there?" she asked the kids.

Bob groaned. Not this again.

All three of them started shouting at once:

"Big bubbles, talent show, karoke, scanger hunt, puppets, paint rocks, tampoline, dancing, hula hooping, gymstatics!" Cindy called out.

"Trampoline, archery, horseback riding, canoeing, tubing, mountain biking, hiking!" Aaron shouted.

"Agility, kayaking, diving, sailing, swimming, tug-of-war, running, ping-pong, volleyball, bungee jumping, zip-lining," Tyler yelled.

Wanda laughed delightedly. She did this on purpose to spin up the kids.

Bob was tempted to cover his ears with both hands. But obviously, he couldn't do that and drive.

And what about fishing? he thought. Bob loved to fish.

Wanda hated it. But Wanda could manipulate with the best of them when she needed to. She'd used Bob's love of fishing against him when she was talking him into this trip.

When it became clear Bob was going to Camp Etenia whether he liked it or not, Bob had comforted himself with the idea that he could wander off and fish on his own. That's when the truth came out. "Well, you won't get to just go off by yourself," Wanda admitted. "They have fishing tournaments, and maybe you can talk the boys into entering one with you."

Why did everything have to be so organized?

The kids kept firing out activities. Bob figured they'd have to stay for about five years to do everything the kids wanted to do, and they were staying for only a week.

"Only." Yeah, right.

Seven days was an eternity.

"Seven days of fun and frolic," Wanda kept saying to him while she was getting everyone ready for the trip. She made it sound like that was supposed to be a good thing.

How was Bob going to survive it?

Camp Etenia, Bob had to admit, was a great-looking place. Or it would have been if it wasn't infested with noisy families.

Nestled in a narrow valley between two tall, wooded mountain ranges topped with craggy rock, Camp Etenia hugged the edges of a massive, meandering deep blue freshwater lake, Lake Amadahy. According to the camp brochure, *Amadahy* was Cherokee for "forest water." That would have been an appropriate name for a lake in the woods, except for the fact that the camp was nowhere near Cherokee territory. When Bob pointed that out to Wanda, she didn't seem to care.

Accessed via a ten-mile dirt-and-gravel road that left the highway at the bottom of a steep grade, Camp Etenia didn't announce itself until you were almost upon it. Then an understated rustic sign nearly hidden behind a maple tree reassured tired travelers they were in the right place: CAMP ETENIA: JUST AHEAD.

The camp itself was as picturesque as its surroundings. The main lodge was a huge log cabin flanked by two stone chimneys and an ample porch that ran along the front and sides of the building. The structure was covered with a shiny green metal roof. The camp's thirty-five cabins looked like the lodge's children; little log-and-stone buildings were scattered near the main lodge like baby ducks swimming around their mom. Bob and his family were slated to be in cabin #17, Cabin Nuttah. *Nuttah*, apparently, was an Algonquin name meaning "strong."

Bob's boys thought that "Nuttah" was a hilarious name. "We're going to stay in a nut house," Tyler had told all his friends when they'd gotten their assignment.

"Don't mess with my Nuttah," Aaron kept saying.

"Will it have lots of peanuts in it, Daddy?" Cindy had asked several times.

Wanda said, "We'll get nutty!"

Bob responded, "I'm going nuts."

He thought the name was idiotic because, again, the Algonquin tribe lived nowhere near here, either. The owners of Camp Etenia seemed to have reached into a swirling vortex of Native American names and randomly picked a few.

Camp Etenia's parking lot was a shady, tree-guarded gravel rectangle behind the main lodge. When Bob pulled the minivan into the lot, he was reminded you couldn't drive your car to your cabin.

"That would ruin the ambiance," Wanda said when Bob complained about it.

"Is excruciating back pain from lugging all our crap also part of the ambiance?" Bob asked.

Wanda smiled at him and applied fresh lip gloss.

Well, I guess that answers that question, Bob thought.

Now that he stood here next to a minivan crammed with luggage and toys—not to mention a cargo carrier stuffed with more of the same—Bob's back started throbbing just at the *idea* of getting everything to the cabin. And of course, Cabin Nuttah was the farthest one from the parking lot.

"It's right at the edge of the woods, Bob," Wanda had gushed when the cabin was assigned to them.

"Oh joy and bliss," Bob said.

And here they were. One woman's heaven was another man's hell.

Bob looked up at the traitorous sky, which had traded its clouds for vast expanses of pale blue. The sun was almost directly overhead, and it shined down with ferocity. Bob figured it was at least eighty degrees, and the air felt heavy and muggy.

Their feet crunching over the gravel, Wanda and the kids were practically dancing around the car. Cindy was spinning in circles, Aaron was doing some kind of dance, and Tyler was drumming on the minivan's hood. Wanda was calling out, "Hi," and "How are you?" to everyone within earshot.

"Look, utterflee!" Cindy squealed.

Bob followed the direction of Cindy's plump pointed finger and saw a monarch butterfly disappear into a clump of salmonberry bushes. He flashed back to his childhood, remembering when his dad took him camping and they picked salmonberries to go with their fried fresh trout dinner.

"Come on, Dad," Aaron said, "we have to get signed up, or we'll miss out on all the good stuff."

"Bob, why don't you go take care of all that." Wanda handed Bob four sheets of paper, covered with lists.

He knew the lists were the activities each child had chosen and the ones Wanda had decided they'd do as a family. He sighed. It was going to take all afternoon to do this.

"The kids and I will go scope things out and start meeting people," Wanda said. "When you're done with the sign-up, you can bring stuff to the cabin."

"Oh, I can? Goody," Bob muttered.

"What's that, honey?"

"Nothing."

Bob watched his family scamper off, but he didn't move. He wished he could just get in the car and drive away. He looked at the driver's seat. What would happen if he did that?

The sweet scents of wildflowers warred with pungent exhaust smells, but overpowering both, the powerful aromas of juniper and pine commanded attention. They made Bob think of a gin and tonic, his favorite drink. "It tastes like an evergreen tree," Wanda had said the first time he made her one. After that, she started calling gin and tonic "that tree drink," and eventually, she shortened it to "a tree." "Make me a tree," Wanda would say occasionally after the kids were asleep on Friday nights.

He could use "a tree" right about now.

Suddenly he got shoved from behind. A kid yelled, "Sorry," as Bob staggered into the side of his minivan. Clutching the open second-row door, he noticed an overweight, sweating, middle-aged man wrestle with multiple duffel bags and suitcases. The man met Bob's eye, and Bob gave him a sympathetic smile. Then Bob shut the minivan's doors and looked around.

He was immediately sorry that he did.

Taking in the camp from behind the driver's seat and watching his family spill from the minivan with uncontained enthusiasm had been bad enough. Seeing the whole of this purgatory in one wide angle was practically unbearable.

Kids ran all over, like they'd been given a drug that

rendered them senseless but kept them in perpetual motion. Men were morphing into pack mules; sweating dads staggered around under the weight of their burdens. Moms were socializing and organizing. In the midst of the chaos, camp counselors blew whistles and shouted incomprehensible instructions.

Bob tried to decipher what they were saying, but he couldn't. Steeling himself, he approached a pony-tailed blonde, blue-eyed counselor. She blew her whistle when he was just four feet away from her. The high-pitched screech catapulted into his ears and zigzagged around his brain for several seconds before he could speak.

"Excuse me," he said, "but which way to sign up for activities?"

Ridiculously, she blew the whistle again, but this time it was at least a short burst, and she pointed to a shallow flight of stairs on one end of the lodge. "Go up those stairs, and follow the walkway to the front porch. Get in the line, and it will lead you to the sign-up tables inside." She blew the whistle again.

Bob's fingers itched to pull the whistle off her neck, but he contained himself.

"Thanks," he said through a murderous smile.

Bob went up the stairs and found the line on the lodge's front porch. From here, he could see that his family was already settling in. Cindy was holding hands with another girl, this one with black braids, and spinning around on a big dock that stretched over the lake. What was it with little kids and spinning? Near Cindy, Wanda was talking to a woman while Bob's boys and another boy took turns trying to skip rocks across the surface of the lake.

And here he was, standing in a line so he could take care of paperwork. Story of his life.

Bob lost track of how long he waited. Flies droned around his head, and he felt his nose starting to burn. That would teach him to ignore Wanda's advice to put on sunscreen.

"It's going to rain," he'd told her confidently.

"You never know," she'd said. It was amazing how often she *did* know what he didn't know.

Someplace nearby, someone played a guitar. Someplace even nearer, someone ate beef jerky. Bob wrinkled his nose. The smell made his stomach roil.

Other parents were chatting in line, but Bob kept his head down. For the first time since he'd pulled the minivan out of his driveway, he was able to think about the proposal he wished he was home working on. He didn't have time to take a week's vacation, and if he did, he sure didn't want to take it running himself ragged doing *activities* with a bunch of strangers. Honestly? He needed to be alone.

Bob turned to watch his family again. Cindy and her new friend were now playing a makeshift game of hopscotch between the lawn and the lake, while the boys were trying to balance on the pilings along the edge of the dock. He was sure he was going to hear a splash pretty soon.

Bob finally reached the doorway of the lodge. Hard to believe, but it would eventually be his turn. Curious in spite of himself, he looked around the lodge's interior. It was just as the brochure depicted: exposed log walls, lots of big heavy wood furniture padded with cushions covered in vaguely Native American patterns. A massive buck's head presided over the fireplace, and the chandeliers hanging from the log roof were made of antlers. This was not the best place to be a deer.

Bob took one last peek at his family before he stepped completely into the building. As expected, the boys fell into the lake. Cindy continued to play hopscotch. Wanda laughed at her sons . . . only because they were laughing, too.

If anyone had asked Bob if he loved his family, he would have answered a vehement "Yes!"—because he did. But that didn't mean he *liked* them all the time, and lately, he'd been liking them less and less. They always wanted something.

Daddy, look at the picher I drew, Cindy would say.

Dad, can you throw the ball to me? Aaron would ask.

Dad, please help me with my school project, Tyler would beg.

Honey, the garage door is rattling; please fix that, Wanda would order. Yeah, *order*. She always said "please" but it felt no less like an order than it did when his boss said, "Get that done today, *please*."

Bob was tired of all the requests, all the obligations. He needed to *breathe*.

"It's your turn, dude." Someone tapped Bob on the shoulder.

He looked around.

A young dad who obviously still loved fatherhood stood behind Bob. The dad grinned and pointed over Bob's shoulder. "You're up."

At the table in front of Bob, a hefty, tanned woman with super-short dirty blonde hair and smile lines around her eyes looked up at him. "Hi. I'm Marjorie." She gave him a big smile, and he admired her very white, even teeth while she pointed to the white plastic name tag pinned to her green Camp Etenia shirt. "Welcome to Camp Etenia."

"Oh, is that where I am?" He was aiming for dry humor, but apparently he missed the mark.

Marjorie's smile faltered. She frowned for a second and then said, "Name?"

"Mackenzie."

The woman tapped the keys on a wireless laptop. "Bob, Wanda, Cindy, Aaron, and Tyler."

"That's right."

"Okay, let's get you signed up. Have you prepared your list of activities?"

Bob handed the woman Wanda's neat lists. The camp offered 112 activities and asked that campers come prepared with lists of at least twenty, ordered by preference. Wanda's lists held seventy-two activities altogether. Bob wondered what Marjorie would do with that.

But she didn't seem surprised at all. "Perfect," Marjorie said as she began typing.

Bob watched her, his jaw clenched. One of the objections he had to Camp Etenia—in fact, to any summer camp—was the rigidity of the whole thing. He had no issues with being outdoors or doing fun things, but doing things on a schedule, following a list—that drove him nuts. Ha! Maybe he *did* belong in Cabin Nuttah.

Seriously, though, didn't he get enough schedules and lists to follow at work? At least at work he was getting paid. Why did he have to be subjected to this crap at home, too?

Marjorie stopped typing. "I wasn't able to get you into every activity listed, but I managed the top twenty for each of your children and for your family as a whole."

"Awesome juice." Bob enjoyed using one of Tyler's favorite sayings. Tyler actually meant it when he said it, but for Bob "awesome juice" meant either "That sucks" or "I couldn't care less."

Marjorie handed Bob's lists back to him, then looked both ways and behind her before leaning forward. When she spoke, her voice was barely above a whisper. Bob heard "Do you want," but the rest was incomprehensible.

He leaned forward. "I'm sorry?"

Marjorie leaned forward, too. Her breath smelled like chocolate. "Do you want to sign up for a Bunny Call?" she asked.

He must have misheard her. Bob asked, "What's that?"

Marjorie turned and pointed toward a tall rabbit standing in the far corner of the massive room, under an antique canoe hanging from the vaulted ceiling. The rabbit, which had bright orange fur, wore a white-and-black checked vest, a yellow-and-white polka-dot bow tie, and a black top hat, through which its floppy ears stuck straight up. The rabbit held cymbals, like old-fashioned windup monkeys used to have. Bob blinked. How had he missed the rabbit when he first looked around? It was like missing an anaconda in a pen full of puppies. The rabbit did not belong. It really did not belong.

Bob was mesmerized by the rabbit for several seconds. He couldn't tell if the rabbit was a person wearing a costume or one of those creepy animatronic things he'd seen in a couple of restaurants his family had visited when he was young. In any case, it wasn't the kind of rabbit that made you want to cuddle up to it. Its eyes were a little too big to be friendly; they bordered on crazed.

"Mr. Mackenzie? Bob?"

Bob blinked. "Huh?"

Marjorie grinned at him and winked. "When you sign up for a Bunny Call, the rabbit over there—his name is Ralpho—will visit your cabin."

Bob looked back at the rabbit, Ralpho.

"He'll come into your cabin screaming, clashing cymbals, and spinning his head." Marjorie chuckled. "It's really something terrifying to behold!"

Bob could just imagine it.

"It's quite the wake-up call," Marjorie added.

Bob didn't get it. "Wake-up call?"

"Oh, right, I didn't say. Ralpho makes his rounds between five a.m. and six a.m. During that hour, he'll visit every cabin that signs up for a Bunny Call. It's a bit of a naughty prank we play on the children on their first day here. Most of them love to have that rush of terror when they're scared silly first thing in the morning." Marjorie chuckled again. In her low voice, the sound was reminiscent of a villain's devilish laugh. "Are you interested?"

Bob looked from Marjorie to Ralpho and back again. He thought about his annoyingly happy family and their insistence that he spend his only week off this summer in this poorly disguised detention center for overworked dads. He thought about how long he'd stood in this stupid line signing up for all the asinine activities. He thought about all the luggage he still had to schlep to Cabin Nuttah.

Then he thought about how his family reacted to loud noises in the morning. That thought began teasing some of his good humor to the surface.

"Sure!" He grinned. This was going to be a riot!

"Wonderful," Marjorie said. She tapped her keyboard again. "There. All signed up." She smiled up at him, and he smiled back.

It was Bob's first genuine smile of the day. It was the first moment since this trip had been scheduled that he felt something other than resentment and annoyance. He even felt a little delighted.

Marjorie leaned over to grab a stack of papers she'd just printed. She thrust them in front of Bob. "If you could read these over to be sure you approve, and then initial each page." She handed him a pen. He sighed and read the excruciating lists one more time. He didn't approve at all, but he initialed the pages anyway.

Marjorie beamed. "Excellent!" She shuffled the papers, and stapled some of them together. "Here are your schedules," she said. "Ralpho will visit in the morning, and the rest of your activities are blocked out on the calendar." She handed Bob a key and a little booklet. "Key to Cabin Nuttah and a book of camp rules," she explained.

Oh lovely. A book of rules. Bob needed more rules . . . like he needed a few more jobs or a few more kids.

He didn't say that out loud. He just took the rulebook and the key.

"Have fun, and don't hesitate to ask if you need anything," Marjorie said.

Bob nodded at her, gave Ralpho one last look, and then headed outside. He noticed his step felt lighter. He was tempted to do a little spin as he headed out the door. Instead, he turned to Ralpho one last time and tipped an imaginary hat to his new "friend."

"Thanks, buddy," Bob said quietly. Ralpho had given Bob the most profound sense of gratification he'd had in weeks.

Bob hauled the last load of luggage into Cabin Nuttah and stepped back outside to catch his breath. Basically an A-frame with a shallow porch, Cabin Nuttah was a simple log structure with two small side windows, one picture window in the front, and a small window on the loft level.

Bob shook his head at the cabin. It wasn't the five-star hotel he had envisioned spending his vacation in.

"Bob?" Wanda called.

He went inside the cabin, and Wanda gave him what he'd come to think of as "the look." The look was a *lips-quirked-to-the-side-with-an-eyebrow-raised* expression that meant "You're not doing what I want you to do."

"What?" Bob asked.

"You need to get a move on. It's time for the Opening Day Picnic," Wanda complained, bustling over to Bob and waving the schedule under his nose. "See? Four p.m. We're going to be late."

"No one is on time for picnics," Bob said.

Wanda threw a pair of khaki shorts and a navy-blue polo shirt in his direction. "Here. Change into these. You smell like sweat."

"You think?"

Wanda's words had sounded accusatory, and he wanted to ask her how he was supposed to have gotten all their stuff to the cabin without working up a little sweat. Instead, he watched Wanda set up Cindy's "sleeping kit," a small vinyl pouch tucked into a white wicker basket. The pouch held a sleep mask and earplugs, and the basket included a cup of water with a lid.

From early in their relationship, Bob had known that Wanda was a loud snorer—she'd fallen asleep on his shoulder at an outdoor concert once, and her snores were somehow audible over the loud music. When they had kids, he found out that the snoring thing was genetic, and unfortunately it came with a propensity toward light sleep and an overreaction to being awakened by loud noises or bright light. These days, Wanda and the kids all wore earplugs and blackout sleep masks to bed. Bob never bothered with a mask, but Wanda's snores forced him to wear earplugs, and even those weren't enough to keep him from feeling like he spent every night in a working sawmill. That was another thing about this trip that displeased him: All four of his snoring family members in one small area? Bob didn't see a lot of sleep coming his way over the next seven days. One of the reasons he got such a kick out of the Bunny Call was he thought it would mete out a bit of justice. If he had to be tortured all night, at least they'd get a little shock in the morning.

Cabin Nuttah was as basic on the inside as it was on the outside. On the first floor, the cabin held a double daybed with a pull-out trundle bed beneath, a table with five chairs, a chest of drawers, and a small refrigerator. A door led to a tiny bathroom. Up in the loft, two twin beds with matching nightstands were tucked under the roof's steep pitch. The cabin had no shelves or closets. Instead, coat hooks lined several of the walls, and low benches were set under the hooks, presumably to hold luggage. Wanda had already stashed all of their suitcases neatly in rows. She'd also piled snacks, paper plates and cups, and a roll of paper towels on top of the refrigerator.

"I thought there would be bunk beds," Aaron had said

when Bob reached the cabin. "Bunk beds would have been fun."

"When I was your age, your uncle and I were complaining that we *had* to have bunk beds," Bob told his son. "We thought twin beds would have been fun."

"Yeah," Aaron said, "but you're old."

Bob wondered what that had to do with it. He didn't think of himself as old, although with each passing day the label got closer to sticking. But even if he was old, did old automatically mean wrong? He was beginning to think it did.

Bob surveyed the cabin's beds, indulging in a moment's anticipation for the Bunny Call. Every bed in the cabin was covered in a red blanket, and the sheets were dark green. This gave the place a decidedly Christmassy feel that was heightened by the green-and-red striped curtains on the windows. Bob thought it was a little weird and had said so when they first entered the cabin, but Wanda had insisted, "It's festive."

"Exactly my point," Bob had said.

Although the boys didn't like the lack of bunk beds, they did like one of the cabin's features: it had a trapdoor in the floor.

"What's that for?" Aaron asked when he found it.

Bob made Aaron wait while he dropped through the trapdoor and checked out what was below. Turned out it was just the cabin's crawl space. Bob figured they'd decided to put the crawl-space door inside to prevent critters from getting under the cabins. Or maybe it was an insulation thing. Whatever it was, it delighted the boys, who went in and out of the crawl space several times, jabbering about hidden treasure.

Wanda snapped her fingers in front of Bob's face. "Why are you just standing there?" She gave him a push. "Change!"

Obediently, Bob began peeling off his sweaty clothes, replacing them with fresh ones. When he was done changing, he stood at mock attention in front of his wife, who had already changed into a simple emerald-green sundress. "Do I pass muster?"

Wanda smiled, gave him a hug, and kissed him on the cheek. She recoiled. "Oh. Rough. You need to shave."

"I'm on vacation," Bob reminded her.

"That's an excuse to give your wife whisker burn?"

Bob sighed. Would he ever get a break from anything? He picked up his shaving kit.

"Not now!" Wanda said. "We're late."

Bob dropped the kit in frustration. "Well then, you just tell me exactly when and where and how, and I'll do exactly what you want," he said.

Wanda didn't seem to hear the acrimony in his words. She probably thought he was serious, because she smiled at him, and linked her arm through his. "Let's go to a picnic."

Spread out over a vast expanse of lawn sloping down to a sandy beach, the picnic was a chaotic mass of food, games, and socializing. Bob wanted to run and hide in the forest the second he and his family reached the edges of the tumult.

CAMP ETENIA WELCOMES YOU! a bright-green banner shouted from its place stretched between two massive fir trees. Bob doubted that Camp Etenia welcomed any of them. It was more probable that the camp wanted them all to go away. In fact, Bob was pretty sure Lake Amadahy wished the camp had never been built.

Bob had entered the architecture firm as an apprentice right out of school, and in the twelve years he worked there, he'd learned a lot about form and function and energy and landscape. Walking sites to prepare plans, he often had a sense of when a place welcomed a structure and when it didn't. Not that he ever shared that tidbit with anyone. He kept his intuitive sense of a place in mind when he designed structures, but he never told his clients he was repositioning a building on a site because the earth wanted it that way. He had some sort of weird sense about land and nature, but he wasn't stupid.

"Come on, Bob." Wanda tugged on his arm. "Stop loitering. You look like a deer in headlights."

"I *feel* like a deer in headlights. I'll probably be mounted on one of the lodge walls by the end of the week."

"Very funny." Wanda towed Bob to the end of a row of picnic tables. They were lined up, covered with dark-green vinyl cloths, and valiantly trying to hold several tons of food. Wanda handed him a heavy-duty paper plate. "We might as well eat while the kids play. Then I'll corral them and help them get their own meals."

Bob looked around for the kids. The boys appeared to have become ninja warriors. They wore green headbands now, and they were having sword fights with long sticks.

He glanced toward a cluster of toddlers clambering around a clown, who was smearing paint on a redheaded girl's face. Cindy was hopping up and down next to the girl. "Me too. Me too," she squealed loud enough that Bob could hear her clearly from a great distance. "Make me buzzy honeybee," Cindy commanded.

Bob winced and turned back to the food. He hated clowns.

"Doesn't it smell good?" Wanda gestured at the platters of potato salad, bean salad, macaroni salad, pasta salad, green salad, deviled eggs, raw veggies and dip, chips and dip, baked beans, and various casseroles that were covering the picnic tables.

"Honestly? All I can smell is burnt hot dogs," Bob said.

A barbecue was set up halfway between the food tables and the lodge. From the charred smells and the flames belching into the air far too high for safety, Bob wasn't sure the "chef"—a skinny camp employee with a narrow, flushed face—knew what he was doing.

Wanda wrinkled her nose. "The hot dogs are why I encouraged Cindy to get her face painted. But really, can't you smell the dill in this salad? And the thyme in this one? Give them a chance."

"Woof," Bob said before dutifully sniffing the salads. He still couldn't smell anything except overcooked barbecue.

Wanda giggled. "Come on. You're holding up the line."

Bob sighed and started dishing up the salads. While he piled food on his plate, he tried not to dread the inevitable scene that would unfold when Cindy realized there were hot dogs being consumed all around her.

Cindy thought hot dogs were "cru," i.e., cruel. "Can't eat doggies!" Cindy had protested the first time hot dogs were presented to her. No manner of explanation convinced her that the term "hot dog" was not precisely descriptive of what she was eating.

"Bob?" Wanda gave him a gentle shove. "Honey, whatever you're thinking about you can think about later. Come on." Wanda led him to a long picnic table filled with laughing couples.

"Are these seats taken?" Wanda asked one of the couples.

"No, they're all yours," a large, boisterous woman with big hair and a mouth to match sang out. "Pull up a bench!" She laughed as if she'd just said the funniest thing in the world. Her laugh was a high-pitched trill that sounded like a bird's mating call.

Her husband, a small, sandy-haired man with sunburned ears, glanced up and offered an unconvincing replica of a smile. Bob matched it with his own social tooth-baring. Wanda plopped down on the bench and scooted in to make room for Bob.

"I'm Darlene," the large woman said. "And this is Frank." She pointed at the guy with the sunburned ears.

Frank lifted a fork, then returned to eating.

"Don't mind him," Darlene said. "When he gets food in front of him, he forgets how to talk. Eats like a horse, my Frank, and look at him. It's not fair. I eat a carrot, and I gain a pound."

Bob had no idea what to say to that, so he let Wanda handle it. He heard her say something sympathetic while he put his attention to his food.

The bench was hard and narrow, and it hurt his butt. He shifted, and he whacked his knee on the picnic table frame. He shifted again, and a splinter the size of a small knife jabbed him in the thigh. A pair of flies dive-bombed his plate, and he shooed them away.

This was supposed to be fun?

He stabbed a chunk of potato and stuffed it in his mouth. It wasn't cooked all the way through. He hated crunchy potatoes in potato salad. He made a face as he chewed, wishing he could spit it out, wishing he could spit out this whole miserable experience.

While Bob ate, an animated conversation about camp activities began. Everyone at the table offered an opinion about what was going to be the most fun thing to do at Camp Etenia. Even Frank, who had finished eating, joined in with apparent glee when he talked about the tennis tournament that would start the next day. When Wanda piped up to tell everyone that their whole family was competing in a capture the flag competition the next day, Bob almost groaned out loud. He'd forgotten he'd agreed to that. The very thought of running around the woods trying to grab a piece of cloth made his teeth hurt. Bob had hoped that after the picnic, he could spend the rest of the day sitting in a deck chair, but he was reminded why he rarely bothered being optimistic. The picnic ended at six, and Wanda informed him that their family was signed up for team competitions from six to nine—in darts, horseshoes, and the card game Hand and Foot. After that, there would be a big campfire and marshmallow roast.

"It's going to be great fun," Wanda chirped a little later as she cleaned up the ketchup smeared on Cindy's face.

Predictably, Bob's family finished last in darts and horseshoes, and seventh in the Hand and Foot tournament, but Tyler was the only one who had a problem with that. Luckily, his disappointment didn't last long. Tyler was like his mom; he didn't dwell on what he couldn't change. He just moved on to the next possibility around the corner.

"That's what life is all about, Bob," Wanda always told him. "Possibility. Every day is filled with possibility. You just have to look for it."

Bob had thought this was adorable for the first few years he was with Wanda. Now it was grating on him . . . maybe because he wasn't seeing a lot of possibilities that pleased him.

This one, for instance, wasn't high on his "good times" list.

The evening's campfire was a massive conflagration expelling smoke that hung in choking swirls over the entire lawn and beach. Bob's eyes burned, and his throat felt raw.

"Look at the big fire, Daddy!" Cindy said, tugging on his hand so they could move closer.

Bob had instinctively grabbed Cindy's hand as soon as he'd seen the fire. She loved bright things, and he knew she'd make a beeline for it, which she did.

"Fire's hot, sweetie," he said. "We'll look at it from over here." He tried leading her to a pair of lawn chairs well away from the flames, but she was having none of it.

"No! Fire! Roost smallows!" Cindy demanded.

Wanda took Cindy's other hand. "I'll take her. You go sit."

Bob let go of Cindy's hand. "Thanks."

Wanda blew him a kiss and trotted with Cindy toward the marshmallows and crackling fire. Bob turned toward the lawn chairs, but of course they were all taken now. He scanned the area for a place to sit. Sighing, he went toward one of the logs set up around the campfire and awkwardly perched on the curved edge.

A mosquito immediately appeared and landed on his knee. He smacked his knee and killed the mosquito. "I thought you guys didn't like smoke," he said to the dead bug.

"I think they get used to it," a balding man with a big gut said as he dropped onto the log next to Bob. "Maybe they build up a tolerance in places like this." His voice was deep and smooth. He could have been a radio personality.

"Think so?" Bob said noncommittally. He held out his hand. "Bob Mackenzie."

"Steven Bell." The man shook Bob's hand. "Actually," he said, "I think my theory's full of it. Mosquitoes don't live long enough to build up a tolerance. Did you know that the average female mosquito lives about fifty days and the average male lives about ten days?"

"Figures," Bob said. "The females and the babies never leave them alone."

Steven laughed. "You got that right." He gestured toward a pair of very pretty blonde girls Bob guessed were thirteen or fourteen. The girls were flirting with a couple teen boys wearing pants so baggy they were about to fall off. "Or they worry themselves to death. Those two girls are mine." The guy shook his head. "I don't sleep much."

Bob nodded. "I can see why."

"You have girls?"

"One. She's just three. Two boys, too."

"Fatherhood's not for the faint of heart," Steven said. "But it's a heck of a lot of fun."

Bob offered a socially acceptable nod that didn't represent at all what he was thinking.

It was nearly 11:00 p.m. by the time the whole family was back in the cabin and the kids were ready for bed. The boys said good night and fell into their twin beds, asleep almost the second they hit the mattresses. Their snores began vibrating the exposed ceiling beams immediately.

Cindy, on the other hand, was wound up. Wearing one of the cabin's extra quilts as a cape, she was dancing around the place shouting, "I'm a princess!"

"If you're a princess, where's your crown?" Bob asked.

"Oh, now you've done it, Bob," Wanda said.

And sure enough, Cindy started crying because she didn't have a crown.

"Oops," Bob said.

It took Wanda several minutes to convince Cindy they could make her a princess crown during crafting time the next day. In the meantime, Cindy had an invisible crown.

"Okay," Cindy finally said.

Wanda and Bob sighed in relief.

Cindy still wasn't ready to go to sleep. "Story!" she begged, crawling into Bob's lap.

Bob sat with his back against the metal frame of the double daybed. He was pretty sure the frame, in a previous life, had been a medieval torture device. It managed to attack both his spine and his kidneys at the same time.

Bob wrapped his arms around Cindy and tried not to inhale her smoky scent. Normally Cindy smelled like strawberries and vanilla at night—the strawberry scent was from her shampoo and the vanilla was from the warm vanilla almond milk she liked to drink before bed. Wanda decided to skip the kids' bath time tonight because the day had been so long, and Cindy was already feeling "bloopy" from too many "smallows" to make room for her usual before-bed treat.

Bob watched Wanda open the window on the far side of

the cabin. She was fanatical about having fresh air in the evening, no matter how cold it was outside. At least it wasn't that frigid tonight.

Wanda crossed the cabin, pulled back the covers, and slid in next to Bob. She looked at her daughter. "Okay, what story are we doing tonight?" she asked Cindy.

This was the routine. Bob held his daughter, and Wanda told the story. Bob could design and even build houses, but he couldn't put together a story to save his life. Wanda was the storyteller.

"Catpiller!" Cindy shrieked pretty much right into Bob's ear.

He cringed but didn't push her away.

"Okay." Wanda leaned over and kissed the top of Cindy's head. She sneezed, then nestled close to Bob, laying her head on his shoulder. From there, she began to tell a convoluted story about a caterpillar who built his cocoon all wrong and had to redo it so he could become a butterfly. At one point, Bob was tempted to insert a couple architectural details regarding the building process, but he wisely remained silent.

At the beginning of Wanda's story, Cindy kept piping up with her opinion about how things should go. Every time she did, she squirmed and ended up elbowing Bob in some sensitive area of his anatomy. It was like trying to cuddle with a small kangaroo. Bob wasn't a huge fan of the experience. But about five minutes in, she closed her eyes and her body went limp.

This was the part of the night Bob did like. In fact, he pretty much loved it. When Cindy relaxed, her sweet toddler pudge filled Bob's arms with pillowy, warm softness, and then holding her was one of the most sweet and comforting things in the world. Sometimes it was so comforting he forgot who he was and what he had to do the next day. He forgot to be overwhelmed and angry and resentful. It took him back to his childhood, to memories of snuggling his well-worn teddy bear.

"Earplugs," Wanda whispered, holding them out.

Bob took the earplugs and gently inserted them in Cindy's ears while Wanda took care of her own. She gave Bob a kiss on the cheek, put on her sleep mask, and said, "Good night," as she curled onto her side next to him.

Wanda and Cindy started to snore almost simultaneously. Cindy's first whirring blat landed in the same ear she'd shrieked into a few moments before. This time, Bob shifted Cindy in his arms. But he didn't immediately transfer her to the trundle bed. He just sat there, holding his daughter and listening to his family's rumbling snores.

Beyond the snores, the noises of the nighttime forest reached out to Bob's senses; that, combined with the tender sweetness of his family snuggling close, eased the remaining tension in his body. Nighttime in the forest was actually one of the things he'd been okay with about this trip. He remembered lying in his sleeping bag next to his dad, under the stars, listening to the crickets. Ever since then, nature's night sounds had soothed him. Bob tried to hear the crickets now, but all he could hear were Cindy's little popping *splert, splert, fllllbbs* in his ear. That was okay, too.

Wait. Was that an owl?

Bob listened hard. Yes, an owl hooted not too far from the cabin.

Bob's dad, a nature and animal lover, was interested in animal symbolism. He'd taught Bob that owls were often seen as harbingers of death, but they could also be portents of renewal and rebirth. What message did this owl have for Bob?

Bob didn't know, but he did know that for these cherished moments holding Cindy, he could convince himself that he had good things in his life. He could talk himself into the "all is well" mentality Wanda lived out every day.

Suddenly, Bob stiffened. The image of an orange bunny with a white-and-black checked vest flitted through his mind.

Ralpho!

"Oh man," Bob whispered. How could he have signed up his family for such a cruel prank? It was probably going to traumatize Cindy for life.

Listening to the snoring concert going on around him, Bob thought about how upset his wife and kids always were when they were awakened abruptly. Doing that on purpose wasn't the nicest thing in the world. *No, tell the truth, Bob*, he berated himself. The truth was that signing up his family for the Bunny Call was "cru."

What had he been thinking?

He'd been thinking about himself.

Now he thought about his peacefully sleeping wife and kids. However put upon he might feel on this trip, taking it out on them wasn't justice at all. It was selfish and childish.

He sighed. Well, it was too late now.

Hopefully, the Bunny Call wouldn't be so bad.

Bob inched away from his wife and carefully placed Cindy in the trundle bed. Then he put in his own earplugs and lay back on his pillow. In spite of his exhaustion, he lay there a long time before he fell asleep.

Bob sat up in bed and clawed at his earplugs. Digging them frantically from his ears, he felt his heart hammer against his rib cage like it was desperate to get out. Sweat glued his gray T-shirt and boxer shorts to his body.

What in the world?

Usually, Bob didn't sleep all that well, but he wasn't prone to panic attacks or night sweats. So what woke him up?

He looked around the cabin. Was everything okay?

It seemed to be. His wife and kids were snoring in a strangely endearing harmony of buzzing and honking tones. The doors were closed, but through the open window he could still hear the peaceful sounds to which he'd fallen asleep. Nothing appeared to be amiss.

Bob tried to calm his breathing, but it wouldn't slow down. He concentrated to try and remember what he'd been dreaming before he—

Ralpho.

That was what he'd been dreaming about. He'd been dreaming about Ralpho. Obviously his guilt had followed him into his sleep.

Bob took a deep breath and got out of bed. He grabbed the penlight on his key ring.

Bob used his penlight to find safe passage past the end of the trundle bed and then a few feet across the floor to the bathroom. There, he closed the door and turned on the light over the sink. He looked at himself in the mirror. Still the same Bob. Or was he? This Bob looked a little feral. His eyes were bloodshot, and his hair stuck out. His mouth was stretched into a wide grimace. This Bob looked like he'd made a deal with the devil. Had he?

Bob snorted and shook his head. He noticed his eyebrows were getting too bushy. In the last year or so, Bob had started losing hair on top of his head, and he'd started growing hair where he didn't want any extra. How was that fair? Or forget fair. What purpose did it serve?

Leaning over the sink, Bob ran cool water and splashed his face. While his family continued to snore, he thought about Ralpho again. He looked at his watch. It was 11:50 p.m. He'd barely slept before he woke up. This did not bode well for a good night's sleep.

Just over five hours before Ralpho would show up. Could Bob call it off? If he could, how would he do it?

Were the camp counselors available during the night? Yes, he remembered. The cabins had no phones, and Camp

Etenia had no cell phone coverage. But an idle flip through the rulebook had revealed that every cabin was equipped with a large bell you could use to signal for help in case of an emergency.

Bob didn't think this was a bell-ringing emergency. In fact, he was pretty sure if he rang a bell to cancel the Bunny Call, they'd kick him out of the camp.

. . . *then again.*

Bob shook his head. He wasn't going to humiliate his family by ringing an emergency bell to cancel a prank, even if it might get him out of this so-called vacation. Besides, if he did that, they'd know what he'd set up.

Bob leaned over the sink again and slurped some water. Straightening and wiping his mouth, he decided he was making way too much out of a silly prank. Ralpho was just some kid in a rabbit suit, right? All Ralpho would do was scare the kids a little, probably annoy his wife, and that would be that. No big deal. Wasn't part of parenting getting his kids ready for the big, bad world? If they could be undone by a noisy orange rabbit, how did they have any hope of surviving real-world battles, like those Bob faced every day?

Bob nodded at himself in the mirror and turned off the bathroom light. He'd convinced himself that the Bunny Call would be good for his kids. Bob was doing his kids a favor.

And Wanda?

Well, Wanda was a big girl. She could handle it. And if

not, well, she did drag him to this absurd place. A little payback wouldn't be so bad. Would it?

Bob nodded again and headed back to bed.

Bob lay on his side in the dark. How much time had passed since the last time he checked? He pressed the button on the side of his watch, and the tiny light revealed digital numbers informing him a mere nineteen minutes had passed since he'd last compulsively checked the time.

And before that nineteen minutes, it had been twenty-three minutes. Before that, it had been thirty-three minutes. Before that, it was thirty-seven minutes. Before that, it was forty-nine minutes. If he kept up this pattern, he'd be waking up every couple minutes within the next half hour.

Approximately two hours and forty minutes of thrashing in the bed and opening his eyes to check his watch—what a great night Bob was having. Apparently he didn't believe all his rational arguments in favor of the Bunny Call.

Bob closed his eyes and tried to go back to sleep.

Sure enough. The next time he looked at his watch, thirteen minutes had passed. Then seven. And now three.

It was getting close to 3:00 a.m. Two more hours.

One and a half hours.

One hour.

A half hour.

Fifteen minutes.

Five minutes.

His eyes felt like something had been trying to scrape its

way out through his irises all night long. Bob looked around the cabin, but he only saw a whole lot of blackness.

At home, the house was never this dark. Their home had exterior lights, and the subdivision had streetlights.

Camp Etenia's cabins didn't have exterior lights because, according to the camp's brochure, that would "ruin the nature experience." Wanda had brought a night-light from home, but the boys refused to let her plug it in. "It will ruin the nature experience, Mom," they'd said in unison before laughing uproariously.

And so Cabin Nuttah was nothing but a featureless void. If it wasn't for the sounds of his family's snores, Bob could have convinced himself he was alone in a vacuum.

Bob held very still and listened. Was Ralpho on the move? Was he out there someplace? Was he right outside the cabin?

Bob felt his arm hairs stand up and quiver in the dark. "Wuss," he whispered.

He wished he could hear something other than snoring. Ralpho could be right outside the door, and Bob wouldn't know it until the door started to open.

Bob fumbled for his penlight and aimed it at the cabin door. He let out his breath. Okay. Good. He could see what was coming now.

So now what? Should he just wait here for Ralpho to burst in and scare his family half to death?

What kind of dad did that?

Bob threw back the covers and got up.

Wanda snorted and turned over. Cindy made a noise that sounded like a chortle.

Bob shone his light on the door again. Should he check outside?

Yes, you idiot, he told himself. Standing here in the dark wasn't accomplishing anything.

Bob crossed to the chest of drawers between the bed and the window on the right side of the cabin. He felt around in the top drawer for a pair of sweats. Finding them, he pulled them on. Then he went to the cabin door and slipped on the sandals that were neatly lined up with a row of smaller sandals against the wall. He opened the door, tensing because he half expected to be smacked upside the head with a cymbal.

But the cabin's small porch was empty.

Bob looked out at the blackness that surrounded Cabin Nuttah. He glanced up at the sky. No moon. No stars. Apparently, the clouds had come back. But what good were they at night? And where was that rain?

It didn't matter. He was distracting himself from the matter at hand.

Resisting the urge to turn on his penlight, Bob let his eyes adapt to the dark. It didn't take long for him to be able to pick out shapes. He could see the vague outlines of the nearest three cabins, and he also could see the vertical pattern of the woods at the edge of the camp. Between two of the cabins, a handful of distorted shapes baffled Bob until he remembered a rustic playground was situated there.

Bob saw a small spark of light in the playground area. He froze. Was that Ralpho? What if that was Ralpho using a penlight like Bob's?

Bob strained to see in the dark. Then he realized he was looking at the glowing end of a cigarette. Good. Rabbits didn't smoke.

Bob contained a burst of laughter. Rabbits didn't smoke? Was Cabin Nuttah really making him nuts? Ralpho wasn't a real rabbit.

Bob watched the minuscule circle of light. It rose and lowered a couple times. Then Bob realized he could just make out the outline of a man. A man. Not a rabbit.

Closing the cabin door behind him, Bob stepped off the cabin's porch. He headed across the hundred feet or so from his cabin to the lit cigarette.

The early morning air was cool and heavy with the thickly sweet scent of the woods and the fresh scent of recently cut grass. Dew moistened Bob's toes as he walked. Away from his snore-ridden cabin, Bob could hear night sounds more clearly; crickets were industriously chirruping. He also heard the rustle and crack of tree branches bending to the will of the wind that had apparently started blowing during the night. As Bob neared the tiny flicker of light, he heard a man's feet shuffle against rocky ground, and then a loud sigh.

"Hello there," Bob called out softly.

The tiny light jerked.

"Sorry to startle you. I—I couldn't sleep."

Bob listened to a man suck in smoke and then expel it. The smell of menthol made Bob's nostrils twitch.

"Me either," the smoker said unnecessarily.

A flashlight clicked on, and the smoker shined a beam of light on his own face. It made the smoker look sinister, especially with smoke pouring out of his nose, but Bob could tell the guy was probably pretty normal looking in the daytime. He had a thick head of light-colored hair, and he had what might be blue eyes. The eyes, though, looked sad.

Bob flicked on his penlight and shined it on his own face. He chuckled. "Not our best sides, huh?"

The smoker appeared to smile. It was hard to tell. The macabre effects of his flashlight turned the smile into a sneer.

"I'm Bob." Bob offered his hand.

"Phillip." Phillip took the last drag of his cigarette and pinched it out between two fingers before taking Bob's hand and shaking it.

Bob felt a little intimidated by the pinching-a-lit-cigarette move, but he told himself to grow up. Aiming his light around, he saw that Phillip was leaning against the end of the swing set. Bob was tempted to take a seat in one of the swings, but then he'd feel even more like a little boy than he already did.

"You sign up for the Bunny Call, too?" Phillip asked.

Bob's breathing sputtered like a guttering candle. He had to run his tongue around inside his mouth before he answered. "Yeah."

Phillip flicked his lighter on and off, then stuffed it in his pocket. "Probably not my best decision."

His expression seemed a little severe for the situation. Didn't it?

"I've been awake most of the night thinking about it," Bob admitted. He looked at his watch.

"What's the time?" Phillip asked.

"It's 5:08," Bob said.

"Why doesn't time crawl when things are going right?" Phillip asked.

Bob didn't answer. What was the point?

So he stood in the dark with Phillip and listened to the wind. He also listened to the ticking of an imaginary clock. It ticked louder than any real clock Bob had ever heard.

Ralpho could show up at any minute.

The men listened and waited. Bob's intestines felt like battling serpents flailing around inside his belly. Bob was seconds from throwing up, but he managed to get himself under control. The serpent slid back down into his gut, but it didn't stop writhing.

"My mom collected stuff," Bob said.

Phillip shifted at the unexpected words. His back chuffed against the swing set.

Bob was surprised, too. He didn't know he was going to say out loud what he was thinking about. Since he started, though, he figured he'd finish. It was better than hanging out here waiting for an orange rabbit while his anxiety ate him alive from the inside.

"Her favorite collectibles were baskets and china teacups." An image of Bob's mother filled his mind. His mom had been old-school and very feminine. She always wore pastel slacks and floral silk blouses, even on housecleaning day. She always tried to be the perfect wife. She'd kind of spoiled Bob, if he was being honest. He'd thought he'd have a life like his dad's. He'd come home from work, put his feet up, and read the paper . . .

Talk about culture shock. Not that Wanda wasn't a great wife.

Bob remembered he was telling a story. "She kept her most prized baskets on top of the hutch in the dining room, and the teacups were on top of the sideboard that was next to the hutch." Bob paused and listened to the wind. That was the wind, wasn't it?

When nothing appeared out of the night, he continued. "One day, I thought it would be fun to try to see if I could throw my basketball up into one of her baskets. I have no idea why that seemed like a good idea. I was nine."

Phillip didn't say anything.

The sense of urgency Bob had felt since he'd gotten out of bed suddenly multiplied tenfold. He rushed on with his story. "So I toss up the ball in a perfect arc. I'd been practicing, and it lands in the biggest basket. I'm jumping around like I've won a tournament, making all the crowd noises, whooping and cheering. But then the ball starts to tip the basket, and the basket starts to go over. It happens in super slow motion, like a millionth of an inch per few seconds. Or at least that's how it seems. And then the basket is on its side, and the ball is on its way past the other baskets and on down the side of the hutch. I can see what's going to happen, and I'm in motion immediately. But there's no way. No way I can stop it. The ball comes down and lands on the sideboard, scattering Mom's teacups all over the place. All but one of them broke. Mom was devastated."

Bob stopped and cleared his throat. "Once I made the decision, the rest of it was out of my control." He shook his head. "I think I made a decision like that today with that Bunny Call."

A loud half-baying, half-yelping cry sounded in the distance.

Bob and Phillip both whirled around.

Was it the wind?

Or something else?

Phillip coughed, cleared his throat, and said in a smoke-abraded voice, "My mom died when I was five. I hardly remember her. But I remember how my dad was before she died. He was a great dad. Taught me how to throw a ball, always showed me what he was working on when he fixed stuff, read me stories at night. But then after Mom died, my dad . . ." Phillip paused when a keening sound sliced through the camp and speared both men.

Bob's muscles were taut with fear and dread.

Bob didn't think Phillip was going to finish his story, but suddenly Phillip said, "My dad got lost. He just got lost. He couldn't do anything for me anymore. He was all about himself. He turned into a horrid dad." Phillip pushed off the swing set. He powered on his flashlight.

Phillip turned and looked Bob in the eye. "I've become just like him."

Before Bob could respond, Phillip turned off his flashlight and walked away. The night plucked him from Bob's reality and deposited him someplace beyond his senses. Bob was left standing alone with more self-knowledge than anyone would ever want to have.

"That's enough," Bob said.

He was going to stop the Bunny Call.

Bob headed off into the woods, going in the general direction, he thought, of where the last two sounds originated. That same direction as the lodge. Maybe someone would be there, someone who could find Ralpho and cancel the Mackenzie Bunny Call.

It was a hundred yards or so to the lodge, but it felt much farther as Bob attempted to follow, using only his small penlight, the gravel-covered path through heavy forest and past darkened cabins. He started at a walk, but he quickly shifted to a jog, hoping he wouldn't trip on a root or an errant ball or an oar. He couldn't afford to waste time. Ralpho could show up to Cabin Nuttah at any minute. For all Bob knew, Ralpho could be there now!

When Bob broke through the last stand of trees at the edge of the open area in front of the lodge, his shoulders sagged. The lodge was completely dark. It was so dark it looked abandoned. That was crazy, of course. Someone had to be in there.

Bob hesitated in the middle of the dew-drenched sloping lawn. Should he pound on the lodge doors and wake someone up?

A squall echoed through the trees. Bob whipped around to look back at the path he'd come down. He stopped thinking and simply went into action. Jogging again, he retraced his steps until he was about halfway to his cabin. His family. Then he heard a scuttling sound that froze his intestinal serpents and turned his spine to ice.

Was that Ralpho?

Bob aimed the narrow beam of his penlight into the underbrush on either side of the path. The pale white light landed on drooping leaves of a wild rhododendron. The plant seemed to be trembling.

Surely Bob was imagining that.

Of course he was. The wind was just stirring the slick green leaves.

Or was it the wind? The leaves weren't moving in a direction that made any sense.

An abrupt explosion of snaps and crackles stirred up a rustling that seemed to move away at a right angle to the path. Without thinking about the consequences, Bob veered off the path and dove into the thick vegetation. He followed the sounds.

Pop. Crinkle.

Ting.

What was that sound?

Bob stopped abruptly, losing his balance. He threw a hand out to catch himself, and he scraped his palm on rough bark. He turned off his penlight. He listened.

There it was again. Barely there. A slightly metallic rattle.

Was it a cymbal?

Trying to make as little noise as possible, Bob started moving again, following the sounds. They moved steadily away from him, heading toward the edge of the camp . . . heading in the direction of Cabin Nuttah.

But not necessarily *to* Cabin Nuttah. There were at least five other cabins around Cabin Nuttah.

Yeah, keep telling yourself that, Bob thought as he tracked the sounds through the forest. He was moving by feel now, afraid to turn on his penlight again. He had this insane idea that Ralpho was messing with him, playing a scary game of hide-and-seek.

What was Bob dealing with? Was it a camp counselor with a sense of humor or an animatronic with its circuits crossed . . . or something more treacherous than either of those?

Bob forced his brain to power down its thinking centers and focus only on keeping his body in motion. He concentrated on where he was putting his feet. He plowed through the forest the way Wanda mowed through shoppers in an after-Christmas sale. He had one goal: stop the orange rabbit. He would not be deterred from that goal.

But wait . . .

Bob halted next to a massive cedar.

He listened . . .

and listened.

He heard . . . nothing.

Absolutely nothing.

Had he imagined all the sounds he thought he heard?

Or was Ralpho done playing with Bob?

What if Ralpho was getting close to Cabin Nuttah?

What if he was already there?!

Bob thrashed back to the path, and when he reached it, he turned on his penlight to illuminate his way. Then he ran flat-out.

Bob hadn't run since he was on the football team in high school. He'd jogged some, but he never stuck with it. So when he reached the cabin, he could barely breathe. All he could do was open the door and fall inside.

Once there, he firmly shut the door and slid to the floor, his legs splayed out in front of him. He heaved to get air into his oxygen-depleted lungs. He was making so much sucking, gasping noise that he was nearly drowning out his family's snores. Nearly, but not quite.

The import of that hit him. They were still sleeping. All was well.

Bob looked at his watch.

It was only 5:25 a.m.

Bob frowned. How was that possible? It felt like he'd been running around the forest for an hour at least.

Bob shrugged. It didn't matter. What mattered was he was here, and Ralpho wasn't.

The door behind Bob's back vibrated when a knock sounded. Bob whimpered.

He stayed very still. Maybe if no one answered the door, Ralpho would go away.

Another knock. This one louder.

Bob got to his knees. He waited.

Another knock. More insistent.

Okay, playing possum wasn't going to work. Pretty soon, Ralpho would be pounding on the door, and he'd wake up Bob's whole family. Wasn't that what he was trying to stop?

Bob turned, grasped the knob, and opened the door a few inches. He looked out.

It was all he could do not to scream.

Ralpho had been startling to behold from across the huge lobby in the lodge. Close up, Ralpho was just plain alarming. Taking a half step back, Bob braced one foot behind the door, held the doorknob firmly, and blocked the opening with his body. Bob looked up at Ralpho's face. Yes, *up.* Too far up. Ralpho was over six-and-a-half feet tall, just to the top of his head! His ears went up another foot or so. And speaking of his head . . . it was a disturbingly big head, almost the size of one of those exercise balls Wanda liked to sit on.

Bob forced himself not to look away from Ralpho's eyes, even though they were an unsettling bright pink. Ralpho gazed down at Bob and waited.

"Er, Ralpho." Bob's voice cracked like he was barely older than Tyler.

He cleared his throat and tried again. "Ralpho, ah, I'd like to respectfully request that we, ah, cancel our Bunny Call."

Ralpho didn't move.

"I'm sorry you came all the way out here," Bob continued, "and I, ah, appreciate your time, but I've decided a Bunny Call isn't the best thing for my family."

Ralpho was immutable.

"So, like I said," Bob plowed ahead, "with due respect, we won't be needing your services."

Bob held his breath.

One second. Two seconds. Three seconds. Four seconds.

Ralpho slowly nodded, turned, and headed down the steps of Cabin Nuttah.

Bob shut the door, locked it, and leaned against it, sighing deeply. Tears filled his eyes. He couldn't remember the last time he'd been so relieved.

It was over. He'd been able to fix his mistake after all.

Bob sank to the floor again. He sat and listened to the snores. He made a mental note to record these sounds before they left Camp Etenia. He might start using them to de-stress.

"Bob?"

Bob turned his head so fast he smacked it against the door.

He heard Wanda shift on the double bed.

"Where are you?" Wanda asked.

"Over here." Bob turned on his penlight and heaved himself to his feet.

"Why are you up?"

"I'm not sure." Bob didn't shine his light at Wanda to see how his answer went over. He was hoping she was still mostly asleep. Wanda's brain generally didn't turn on fully until she'd been awake for a couple hours.

"Could you aim your light at the bathroom? No need to turn on my light, too. What time is it?" Blankets and sheets rustled. The old box springs under the double mattress squeaked.

Bob checked his watch again. "It's 5:28."

He aimed his light out in front of Wanda. It lit up enough of the room that he could see she had her sleep mask pushed up on top of her head. She didn't look his way, which was a good thing because he had no idea how to explain why he was standing in front of the cabin door.

"Mm. Too early to get up," she said.

"Absolutely."

Bob heard what sounded like shuffling footsteps outside the cabin door. His breath caught, and he tilted his head to listen. Was it just a pine cone blowing across the porch? Maybe that was it.

Wanda went into the bathroom and closed the door. No light showed under the door. He heard her doing her thing, but then he heard the shuffling again.

Sshh, pff, sshh, pff, sshh, pff. It was too rhythmic to be a pine cone. Was Ralpho back?

Bob pressed back against the door. He couldn't have said why. Leaning on the door wouldn't prevent Ralpho from knocking. And if Ralpho knocked while Wanda was awake, the jig was up.

Wanda came out of the bathroom, her gaze steady on the illuminated path of Bob's penlight. She didn't even look at him. "Going back to sleep," Wanda said. "Coming?"

"Be right there," Bob said. *I hope,* he thought.

Outside the door, the sound came closer. *Sshh, pff, sshh, pff, sshh, pff.*

Bob turned into a statue. He had no idea what he should do.

Wanda got back in bed. "Light," she said.

He flicked off his penlight, and he heard her plump up her pillow. She exhaled in contentment.

Something thudded softly against the door behind him. The door moved slightly. Bob shoved his back more firmly to the smooth wood.

Wanda's snores joined the kids' snores.

Next to Bob's hip, the doorknob jiggled.

What the heck?

Bob jumped back from the door and shined his penlight at the knob. He reached a hand out, preparing to grab the knob, fling the door open, and ask Ralpho, or whoever was out there, what he, she, or it thought they were doing. Before he could touch the knob, though, he felt something like a static shock—just a faint charge on the end of his fingertips.

Bob knew it was a warning. He just knew it.

Opening the door would be a very bad idea.

Bob frowned. What? That was ridiculous. He was losing his marbles.

Yes, someone was outside the door. Someone was trying the knob. But that someone was either Ralpho or another camper. Bob could handle either.

Or could he?

A metallic scratching sound came from the door. Bob bent over and listened. Someone was trying to pick the lock.

Goose bumps erupted on Bob's bare arms. Ralpho—or someone—was trying to break into the cabin!

What should he do?

Bob looked around wildly. He needed . . . what *did* he need? A phone? No. No phones here.

The bell! No, that wouldn't work. The bell was outside. It was outside, and it was at the bottom of the porch. Bob would have to get past whoever was trying to break in to get to the bell. A lot of good this emergency bell was!

A weapon. Bob needed a weapon. He swept the cabin with his light. Of course it held no traditional weapons. No guns. No knives. No swords. This was summer camp, not boot camp. Not even a bat—his kids hadn't signed up for softball.

His light landed on tennis rackets and fishing poles. Bob swallowed down a hysterical giggle when his brain offered up an image of him fighting off an orange rabbit with a tennis racket in one hand and a fishing pole in the other.

Bob heard a clink and a click.

Well, he had to do something!

Grabbing one of the ladder-back chairs tucked around the table, Bob tilted it and shoved it under the doorknob.

Just in time.

The door started to open, but it caught against the chair. Bob stared at the chair and the door, and he held his breath.

Something thumped against the door, and the door moved inward an inch, shoving the chair across the smooth wood floor. Bob jammed the chair harder under the knob and held it in place. This stopped the door's movement. But by now, it was open two inches. Breathing fast, Bob shined his light into the gap. He leaned over to get a better look.

The tip of a furry orange paw tried to slide through the opening.

Bob jumped back. At the same time, he hissed, "Go away! I said I wanted to cancel the Bunny Call."

Ralpho didn't seem to care what Bob wanted. He moved his paw back and forth in the door opening for several seconds. Bob prodded at Ralpho's paw with his penlight, wanting to push the paw back out through the door. But Ralpho tried to grab the penlight! Bob snatched the light back, then he hit Ralpho's paw with it. The paw wiggled a little but didn't leave the opening, so Bob punched Ralpho's paw as hard as he could with his fist.

Pain shot through Bob's knuckles, and he saw something

dark and moist appear on the orange paw. Before Bob could figure out what he was looking at, though, the paw retreated from the two-inch space.

Bob took a deep breath and let it out. Okay. Maybe Ralpho would go away now. Bob checked the time. It was 5:36. Surely Ralpho would give up and go visit other cabins with standing Bunny Calls. Bob wondered if he could go back to bed. His eyes felt like they were full of broken glass. How would he take part in camp activities for a full day on no sleep?

A *whump* sounded from under the picture window. Bob whirled in that direction. Ralpho wouldn't try to come through a window, would he? Bob quickly aimed his penlight at the large rectangular glass-covered opening above the table and chairs. He sucked in his breath when his light caught the shadow of a large misshapen head.

"Oh no, no, no," Bob whispered as he leaped over to the window. It was locked, wasn't it?

The window started to open.

No, apparently it wasn't locked. Or it was locked and Ralpho had managed to unlock it. Or locks were irrelevant to Ralpho, just as irrelevant as Bob's request that Ralpho go away.

The window opened farther, and an orange paw reached through. Then an ear.

Why don't you just stand here and watch? That's a good plan, Bob.

Bob's sarcastic self-talk made a point. He needed to

move, so he did. But as he lunged for one of the tennis rackets leaning against the wall, he cut himself some slack. It was, after all, reasonable to be dumbfounded in the presence of a furry orange intruder.

Both of Ralpho's ears and most of an arm were through the window by the time Bob started beating on the ears and arm with the tennis racket. Careful to avoid missing the rabbit and hitting the window, Bob's defensive thwacks were relatively quiet. His family's snores didn't stop.

Neither did Ralpho. Apparently impervious to the blows, Ralpho kept reaching into the cabin.

"Get out!" Bob whispered.

Ralpho didn't respond.

Bob looked at Ralpho's paw, which was just a few inches from Bob's chest. The paw was covered in blood.

What?! Blood?!

Bob stopped pounding with the tennis racket. He shined his light on Ralpho, whose head was now coming farther into the cabin. Bob stared into Ralpho's disquieting eyes. "Are you okay?" Bob asked.

Ralpho stared back at Bob, but he didn't speak.

Wasn't this just a guy in a freaky rabbit suit? Ralpho wasn't *real*, was he?

Ralpho's head slid a little farther inside the cabin.

Whatever Ralpho was, Bob couldn't let him in. So Bob shifted his grip on the tennis racket. Instead of hitting Ralpho more, he used the racket to shove at Ralpho's encroaching head. Grunting, he pushed against Ralpho with all his might. For a few seconds, Ralpho pushed back. It was like a bizarre tug-of-war in reverse. But Bob thought about his sleeping family, and that gave him the extra oomph he needed.

Ralpho fell back out of the cabin. Bob quickly but quietly closed and locked the window. Realizing he was breathing loudly, he took a few seconds to get control of himself. Blowing out a long muted breath, he was pleased when he no longer sounded like a train engine.

How could Ralpho be *bleeding*?

If Ralpho was a guy in a suit, why would he be willing to get *injured* to pull off a prank?

Up until now, Bob's logical brain had been trying to tell him that the effort he was expending to keep Ralpho out of the cabin was beyond preposterous. Whoever was wearing or running Ralpho was being persistent, yes. But it was probably just part of some outrageous joke Camp Etenia's staff played on anyone with the audacity to try and stop the Bunny Call. Bob's sense of urgency, his conviction that he was battling a truly dangerous foe, was more than likely all in his head.

But a bleeding Ralpho put a serious crimp in Bob's theory. What if Ralpho really did want to get inside the cabin and hurt Bob and his family?

Maybe Bob was losing his mind.

But then again, maybe not.

The window on the left side of the cabin started to slide open.

Bob moaned. He'd forgotten Wanda had opened that window.

Bob charged over to the window. Just as Ralpho's bleeding orange paw began reaching through the opening, Bob slapped the window closed, catching the intruding paw. The paw bled more heavily, and it moved, reaching. Bob snatched up the tackle box sitting under the window and slammed the paw with the box. The contents of the box clattered, and the noise made Bob pause. The paw curled back toward the window, and Bob opened the window just enough to thrust the paw back outside with the end of the tackle box. He pushed the window closed and locked it.

Bob shined his penlight around the cabin again. What would Ralpho do next?

Come on, think, Bob admonished himself.

Thinking, though, was a bad idea. If he thought, he'd have to face the fact that it really was Ralpho, a very determined Ralpho willing to bleed to reach his goal, trying to get in the cabin. What else could he want? Bob certainly did not want to think about that. Right now every one of his instincts was telling him to keep Ralpho out at any cost.

This had gone beyond trying to stop Ralpho from *scaring* his wife and kids. This was about stopping Ralpho, period. Bob couldn't have explained what was going on, even if someone had put a gun to his head and demanded he explain himself, but he just knew that there would be horrible consequences if Ralpho got inside the cabin.

Bob tilted his head and listened. He realized he had no idea where Ralpho was. Was Ralpho still outside this window or had he moved on to a different one?

Bob held perfectly still again and listened some more. At first he heard nothing. He checked his watch. It was 5:43.

"Seventeen minutes to go," Bob whispered.

And one more window Ralpho could get through. Why was Bob just standing there?

Outside, the rhythmic shuffling moved past the cabin door. *Sshh, pff, sshh, pff, sshh, pff.* The sound was moving away from Bob. Ralpho was heading toward the other window, the one right next to the double bed where Wanda slept.

Bob knew he had to be sure the next window was locked, but he was rooted to the floor. *Sshh, pff, sshh, pff, sshh, pff.* Ralpho was almost to the edge of the front porch, about to turn the corner.

Bob moved.

He ran through the cabin as lightly as he could, passing his sleeping wife and daughter. Just as he reached the window, it started to move. Bob grabbed the edge of the window and tried to close it.

Ralpho kept trying to open it.

Bob stuffed his penlight in his pocket and used both hands to force the window closed. He concentrated on keeping his breathing even and shallow. He didn't let himself grunt or groan in exertion. He just pushed the window closed while Ralpho pushed the window open.

Stalemate.

How long did Bob stand there straining to close the window? It felt like hours, maybe days. Bob's muscles began to spasm. It felt like his biceps were filled with liquid fire spreading upward into his shoulders. He wanted to scream in pain and frustration.

Outside, faint predawn light was pushing away the blackness. Bob could make out Ralpho's gargantuan head and ears. Bob was just inches from his adversary. Only window glass separated them—window glass and Bob's determination to protect his family. Bob closed his eyes and gave his effort everything he had.

Suddenly, the window slid shut. The *SNICK* of it latching into place seemed impossibly loud.

Wanda stirred, but she didn't wake up.

Weakly, Bob locked the window. Then he dropped his arms and shook them out. They felt like they'd turned into a pair of Cindy's flimsy jump ropes.

Stepping away from the beds, Bob wiped at the sweat covering his face. He felt a ludicrous sense of accomplishment.

A bump and a clatter came from underneath the cabin. Ralpho had moved on.

Bob pulled his penlight from his pocket and aimed it at the floor. The trapdoor!

Bob ran over to the trapdoor and stood on it. He immediately felt like an imbecile. His weight alone wasn't going to be enough to keep the trapdoor closed, at least not if he was standing. Ralpho could easily throw Bob off-balance by opening it. Would sitting on the trapdoor work?

Bob sat down on the door. He listened to the bumps under the floor, growing ever closer. The closer they came, the more Bob thought about how big Ralpho was. Bob wasn't a tiny guy, but he was pretty sure whoever was in the Ralpho suit was strong enough to dislodge Bob from a trapdoor. And then what?

What could he do now? He looked around, grasping for a solution. His gaze landed on the chest of drawers.

Jumping up and running to the chest, he gave it a tentative shove. It was heavy, but it slid easily. The only problem was that the sliding sound was noisy. Cindy's snores paused for a second and then restarted.

Bob's gaze darted around the cabin. *Think, think, think.*

He spotted the quilt lying folded up on the end of the trundle bed. He mentally thanked Cindy for playing with it. If she hadn't, he probably wouldn't have noticed it.

Grabbing the quilt, he lay it on the ground.

Another bump and a scuffle from under the cabin. Ralpho was almost to the trapdoor.

Bob tilted the chest toward him, so it leaned on its side. He let it all the way down to the floor on top of the quilt. Then he bent over, grabbed the edge of the quilt, and started dragging the chest toward the trapdoor as fast as he could.

The trapdoor started to open.

Bob jumped on the door. It closed with a *SNAP* that made Bob wince. But the snoring around him continued.

He leaned back over and grabbed the quilt's edges, hauling the chest toward him as fast as he could. The trapdoor started to rise under his feet again. Quickly, he backed off of it and pulled the chest onto the door. Then he turned the chest onto its back, and he sat on it. The chest started to buck, and Bob felt like he was on some silent malevolent amusement park ride. Was the combined weight of Bob and the chest of drawers going to be enough?

The chest bucked again, and Bob was nearly thrown off. He gripped both sides of the chest and hung on. Bob had never ridden a bull or a mechanical bull, and he wondered if it was like this. His head kept getting yanked around, and he'd have whiplash soon if Ralpho didn't stop.

But Ralpho did stop.

Scuffling sounds under the cabin moved away from the trapdoor and toward the outside wall. Bob slumped on the chest.

Now, was it over?

Bob checked his watch. It was 5:56. Four minutes. Just four minutes. Bob listened closely to the swishing and tapping sounds under the cabin. Ralpho was almost out from under the building.

His whole family was still snoring, but Wanda shifted in the bed. Any of the kids could wake up soon, and Bob didn't want to leave the chest lying in the middle of the floor. After another few seconds of listening, Bob convinced himself Ralpho was no longer under the cabin, so he quickly pulled the chest back to the wall and righted it. He then made a halfhearted attempt to fold the quilt and dropped it on the end of the bed.

Then Bob thought about Ralpho's bleeding paws. Did any blood get inside the cabin? Like on the tennis racket or the tackle box?

Bob decided he didn't want to look. Instead, he trotted to the fridge and pulled off some paper towels from the roll Wanda had put on top. He quickly wiped down both the tennis racket and tackle box; plus, he wiped down all the windows and the floor beneath each one.

Now, wanting very much to climb into bed himself, Bob waited. His instincts were telling him he had to stay alert.

But why?

The cabin was secure. Ralpho was retreating.

A sudden *RAP* drubbed against the back of the cabin.

The back of the cabin? What was Ralpho doing there? Nothing was back there.

No. Wait. The loft window! Bob's stomach and heart switched places. He'd forgotten all about the loft window!

Clamping his penlight in his teeth, Bob climbed the ladder up to the loft as fast as he could, even though every step raised his dread meter higher. He really didn't want to climb up to the loft at all. If Ralpho was up there, Bob didn't know if he could handle it.

But he had to. After all, his boys were also in the loft.

When Bob's head reached the top of the ladder, he hesitated. Then he took a deep, shaky breath. He shined his light at the window on the far wall as he peered up into the loft.

Bob's light revealed the upper half of Ralpho *already through the window.*

Bob let out a choked cry. Thankfully his astonishment cut off the sound in his throat, and his boys snored on.

Gaping at Ralpho, Bob was momentarily paralyzed. This situation was so far beyond anything his mind could process that he felt fully and thoroughly shut down. All Bob could do was stare.

But he had to move. He had to keep Ralpho away from his family.

Why did he just keep gawking?

And suddenly . . . Ralpho paused in his climb through the window. He gazed back at Bob, and neither of them made a sound.

Bob trembled and clutched the loft ladder so hard his hands throbbed.

Outside, dawn arrived, and light shined around Ralpho's orange head, making him look, for an instant, like some kind of supernova monster. Bob was superglued to the ladder. He listened to his own uneven breathing.

And Ralpho began backing out of the window.

Ralpho retreated completely from the cabin. His head dropped below the level of the window.

Then . . .

silence.

Silence all around.

Bob closed his eyes and dropped his head to the top step of the loft ladder.

"Dad?"

Abruptly, the cabin was filled with intense white light. The luminous intrusion into his consciousness felt so invasive that Bob blinked several times and tried to figure out where he was. It felt like he'd been transported to another, otherworldly place.

Bob squinted. He recognized the wide-eyed face of his sleep-rumpled son.

"What're you doing?" Aaron asked. He stood underneath the pull string to the exposed lightbulb that now lit up the loft.

Everything cascaded back into place: the Bunny Call, Ralpho, Bob's frenzied determination to stop the threat to his family.

"What time is it?" Bob asked.

"Huh?"

"The time."

Aaron picked up his cell phone from his nightstand. Really the only function their phones had out here was as a clock.

"It's six," Aaron said.

Tears filled Bob's eyes.

"Dad?" Aaron repeated. "What're you doing?"

Bob ignored him. Now Tyler was sitting up, rubbing his eyes.

"Momma, up!" Cindy's high-pitched voice demanded down below the loft.

"Dad, why are you hanging on to the ladder?" Tyler

asked. He threw back his covers and shifted to the edge of his bed.

Bob didn't know if he could move. He felt like all his muscles had left his body. But he couldn't stay where he was. He didn't have the strength.

So up or down? Up was closer. Bob climbed the rest of the way into the loft. Without answering Tyler's question, because he didn't yet know *how* to answer it, Bob collapsed next to Tyler. He motioned for Aaron to join them.

Looking at his father as if he had grown a second head, Aaron slowly crossed to Tyler's bed. Bob patted the space next to his hip, and Aaron frowned but sat down.

Tyler and Aaron exchanged a look. Then Bob reached around the back of the boys' necks and pulled them both close. He dropped his arms around their shoulders and he squeezed them in a long, tight hug. He wanted to say something, but he was too emotional to talk. He just wanted to hold on to his boys, his precious boys, for as long as . . .

"Dad? You're kind of squeezing the life out of us," Tyler said.

Bob let up on the hug but didn't let them go. He cleared his throat and got his voice to work. "I love you guys," he said. "So much." He looked at both of them in turn.

Both boys had creases on their cheeks from their night's sleep. Their eyes were crusty, and they had sour morning breath. Bob didn't care. They were his sons. They were perfect.

"You know how much I love you, right?" he asked them.

Tyler and Aaron looked at each other again. "Um, yeah?" Aaron said.

"Yeah," Tyler agreed.

"We love you, too, Dad," Aaron said.

A click came from the cabin's first floor, and more light blasted through the little building. Wanda was up.

"Bob, what are you doing up there?" Wanda's scratchy early-morning voice sounded wonderfully normal.

"Come on, boys," Bob said.

The boys didn't move when Bob got up. But Bob grinned at them before heading down the ladder.

What a wonderful morning! It was great to be alive!

At the bottom of the ladder, Bob turned toward the double bed and scooped up his daughter from it. "Cindy Lee, my buzzy honeybee!" he exclaimed before buzzing in her little ear.

Cindy immediately began giggling hysterically. Then she put her arms straight out to her sides and instructed, "Fly, Daddy, fly!"

Bob happily picked her up, and he ran around the room with her, yelling, "Zoom goes the buzzy honeybee. Zoom, zoom. Buzz, buzz."

"Zoom, zoom. Buzz, buzz!" Cindy repeated. Then she let loose with a high-pitched squeal of glee.

"Bob?" Wanda said. She was standing by the bed in her bright yellow silk pajamas, her hands on her hips.

"What?" he asked.

"Something weird is going on."

"What makes you say that?"

Wanda frowned. "I have no idea." She shook her head. "I must have been having a strange dream."

Cindy squealed again. Wanda looked at her daughter . . . and at Bob. Her mouth dropped open and her eyes widened.

The bright light in the cabin brought out the reddest strands in Wanda's hair. Bob couldn't remember her ever being more beautiful. He flew his buzzy honeybee over to his wife, and he engulfed both wife and daughter in a long, tight hug.

"I love you. I love you. I love you," he declared while Cindy said, "Buzz, buzz," and Wanda said, "What's going on?"

Bob didn't answer her. He just squeezed.

"Bee skished," Cindy said. "Ow."

Bob released them. He looked at their gorgeous faces, flushed and smiling. Admittedly, Wanda's smile was tentative, and it was mixed with what appeared to be confusion. But she was smiling.

"Daddy, pee pee," Cindy said.

Bob set his daughter down. Wanda took Cindy's hand and led her into the bathroom.

The second Wanda and Cindy were in the bathroom, Bob looked around the cabin, checking his blood cleanup. He didn't see anything he'd missed.

And what did he do with the paper towels he'd used?

He checked his pockets and felt them there, but he didn't

pull them out because Aaron and Tyler were coming down the ladder. Putting Ralpho out of his mind, Bob hugged his boys again. They tolerated the hugs for a few seconds, until Tyler announced, "I'm hungry."

The bathroom door opened. Cindy, her arms straight out from her sides, started buzzing again. Bob reached out and grabbed Wanda by the hand to pull her close.

"It's a beautiful day and we're together, and we have lots to do today," he said, spinning Wanda into a dance around the cabin.

Wanda laughed. "Who are you and what have you done with my husband?" Then she gave up and allowed him to sweep her up into the dance.

Heading to breakfast at the main lodge, Cindy skipped ahead, but Bob held tight to Wanda's hand.

The sun was already ascending into a brilliant blue sky. The evergreens' boughs were bright green in the morning light, and they seemed to be reaching toward that sky, as if in celebration of the new day. Chickadees played in the forest undergrowth. Their "Fee bee" calls joined with the "Phew chuck" cries of the Western bluebirds Bob could see flitting through the higher tree branches. A woodpecker added a *rat-a-tat* from a tree just out of view. On a low-hanging branch near the trail, a chipmunk chattered, "Spwik, spwik, spwik," as it fluffed its tail. Bob felt like he and everything around him had been cartooned. It all felt too colorful, too cheerful, too, well, cartoony. After everything that had happened the night before, he wouldn't have been surprised if the families around him broke into song.

Camp Etenia was hopping this morning, as everyone was heading to the lodge for breakfast. Kids were running and playing as they went. Aaron and Tyler raced off to join some new friends in a game that involved a lot of shouting. Today, all the activity didn't bother Bob. He was still riding the high of his profound relief.

"I take it you've decided this place isn't so bad?" Wanda asked.

Bob grinned at her. "There are worse places."

Much worse, Bob thought fifteen minutes later as he sat at the table with his family, eating his way through some of the thickest, tastiest pancakes he'd ever known. "Wow. What's in these?" he asked one of the camp employees who came by to top off his coffee.

The perky gray-haired woman leaned over and whispered, "The secret is cinnamon and vanilla, but don't tell anyone I told you." She grinned and bustled off.

Breakfast was being served in the main dining room, which, like the main lobby of the lodge, had a vaulted log ceiling and golden log walls. Bob appreciated that the room was filled with dozens of round tables so families could eat together instead of being forced to join everyone else at long communal tables. The only long table was the one at the front of the room, and it seemed to be reserved for the Camp Etenia staff.

Bob took another bite and watched his kids eat. Aaron and Tyler were stuffing as many pancakes in as they could, acting like they'd never have another chance to eat, ever. Cindy had both pancake and syrup smeared adorably all over her face.

Around them dozens of conversations filled the room with a lively hum that blended with the clinks and clatters of silverware and stoneware. The air was sweet with the aroma of maple and butter.

"Excuse me! Excuse me!" The loud *tink, tink, tink* of a spoon hitting the side of a glass lowered the decibel level in the room partway.

"Could I have your attention, everyone?" Bob and his family, and most of the other diners, looked toward the staff table. In the middle of it, a tall, tanned man with a beard waved at everyone. "Over here," he called. Bob recognized him from the picnic and the campfire the night before.

Talking died down. A few more rustlings and murmurings gave way to silence. Everyone looked at the man.

"Remember me from last night? I'm Evan, the owner of Camp Etenia, and your host. I hope everyone had a good first night."

Bob tensed but kept a smile on his face. Most everyone else cheered.

"Good, good," Evan said. "Okay. A few announcements."

Bob prepared to zone out. He figured Wanda would let him know whatever he needed to know.

"First," Evan said, "regarding the Bunny Calls."

Every cell in Bob's body went on high alert. He tuned in.

"My apologies to those who signed up for a Bunny Call," Evan said.

They should apologize, Bob thought.

"The Bunny Calls couldn't be done this morning because the counselor who usually does Bunny Calls overslept. Ralpho wasn't able to make his rounds today."

Bob stared at Evan.

"These are really great pancakes," Wanda said. "Aren't they, Bob?"

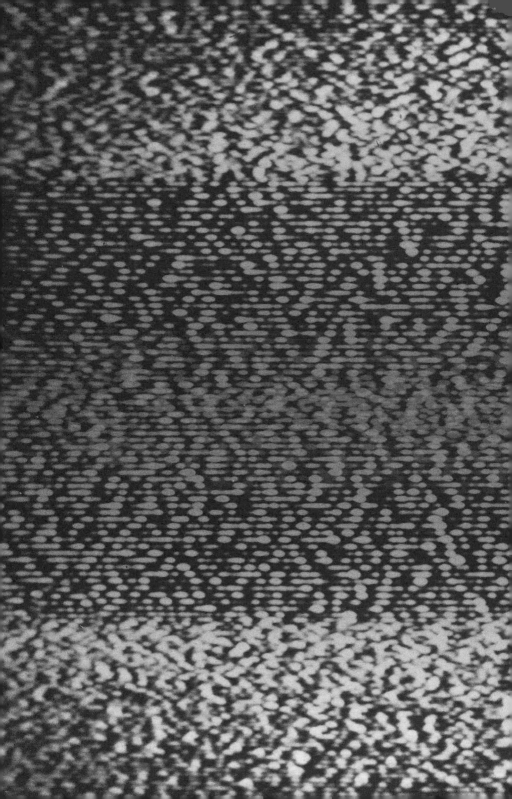

You're so lucky. You just get to sit around and play video games all day."

If Matt had a dollar for every time someone had said this to him, he actually could sit around and play video games all day instead of going into the office and working on developing the things.

Game development was harder than people thought. It was a great job—the job Matt had always dreamed of back when he was a kid pretending to be sick so he could stay home from school and make simple games on his family's home computer. But there was a huge difference between working on games and playing them. Many parts of the process were exhilarating—that first burst of inspiration when an idea came to you, the triumphant moment when you saw all of your plans come to fruition. But between first inspiration and final fulfillment, there were lots of opportunities for head-banging frustration and punching-a-fist-through-the-wall rage. One small programming error could mess up a whole game, and backtracking to try to identify such an error was incredibly tedious. People who loved to play games often thought their skills in gaming gave them the skills to design games as well, but this wasn't any truer than thinking that since you knew how to read a good book, you also knew how to write one.

For now Matt was eating, sleeping, and breathing his job. He had landed the role of creating and refining the AI in *Springtrap's Revenge*, a new cutting-edge virtual reality game that was to be the next installment in the popular *Five Nights at Freddy's* series. It was the most high-profile game he had ever worked on, and he knew it was going to be a tremendous hit. How could it not be, with the exciting combination of virtual reality and the estab-lished *Five Nights at Freddy's* characters that gamers already loved to fear? The early glitches of the game had been worked out, and now Matt was about to do what nongamers assumed the only part of his job was: he was getting to play-test the game.

Matt secured the VR headset over his eyes and made sure the whole device fit him tightly. He was going in.

There was a wall on either side of him. These walls formed the dark hallway that was the entrance to the maze. At this point Matt could only see down the hall straight ahead; no entrances to the left or right were visible yet. Just as he was about to move forward, he saw his creation and his adversary—a large green rabbit—appear at the end of the hall and then exit to the left.

Just because it was a rabbit didn't mean it was cute. Matt had always found humans in rabbit costumes creepy, as was evidenced by an old picture his mom had taken of him when he was three years old, screaming bloody murder on the lap of a blankly grinning Easter Bunny at the mall. Springtrap, the rabbit in the game, was even scarier than the uncanny–valley–dwelling mall Easter Bunny. Its costume was so tattered that some of its mechanical parts were visible beneath the fabric, and the better part of one ear was missing. Its eyes were evil orbs that glowed green when it spotted its prey, and its grin was wide and ghastly. It was definitely nightmare fuel, which was absolutely what Matt had intended for it to be.

Matt was especially proud of his titular character. He wanted to make Springtrap the kind of horrifying character who would endure, who would visit people's nightmares for generations to come. From Dracula to Hannibal Lecter, there was a kind of immortality in a truly horrifying creation, and somehow a bit of this immortality touched the creator as well. Matt had done an exhaustive amount of research in developing the murderous rabbit. He had watched dozens of classic horror movies, studying the personalities of their cold-blooded killers. He read books and articles on serial killers, about how their appetite for violence could only be sated for a little while . . . until they had to choose another victim.

The more Matt watched and read, the more he understood. For the killers who lived on in people's imaginations, murder was a source of joy, a means of self-expression, like painting for the artist or playing an instrument for the musician. Matt wanted Springtrap to show this kind of joy, this kind of deep self-realization, in the art of killing.

He had wanted to create a character who could open your jugular with the same happy excitement as a kid opening a birthday present.

Matt was no murderer, of course. If he were, he wouldn't have had to do so much research. But Matt knew what it was to feel rage—to feel so wronged, so ill used, that he burned with the desire to destroy, to smash, to teach the people who had wronged him a lesson they would never forget. During the game's development, Springtrap became the place Matt could put all these feelings, a repository for all his destructive urges. Springtrap was the child of Matt's rage.

The goal at the beginning part of the game sounded simple: find your way out of the maze before Springtrap can kill you. But the *maze was absurdly difficult, made even more so by the first-person perspective that the VR necessitated. Springtrap was both swift and stealthy and was able to appear seemingly from nowhere and kill you before you knew what hit you.*

Matt made his way to the end of the entrance hallway and decided to turn right since it was the opposite of the direction he had seen the rabbit choose. He ended up, as he knew he would, in a large, square room with four closed doors. Three of these doors led to new passages in the maze. One led to Springtrap and certain death. Because of the way the game was programmed, Matt didn't have any more idea of which door hid Springtrap than any other gamer would. Which door should he choose?

After a quick round of eeny-meeny-miney-mo, Matt chose the door that was straight in front of him. He stepped toward it, turned the knob, and pushed the door open. The soundtrack emitted a deafening screech, and the bunny lunged at him, its arm outstretched, slashing at him with a big, shining knife. The VR made Springtrap's attack feel disturbingly realistic. The knife slashed what felt like dangerously close to his eyes, and when Springtrap lifted the knife high and plunged it downward, Matt couldn't help bracing himself as though he were about to experience real physical pain. Then the perspective shifted to third person so that Matt could see the corpse of his avatar sprawled facedown on the floor. Springtrap, showing the twisted joy that Matt had intended, smiled with a look of true bliss. He knelt beside Matt's avatar and used his knife to slice off Matt's ear. Springtrap held up the blood-dripping ear, a trophy commemorating his achievement. The words GAME OVER *appeared on the screen.*

Matt was furious at himself for choosing the wrong door, furious at his rabbit creation for taking such obvious pleasure in his defeat. He didn't even remove the headset to take a break. He just restarted the game and ran down the hallway until he was in the room with the four doors again. He had a gut instinct that the door on the left was the one to pick.

He approached the door, turned the knob, and pulled it open.

Springtrap lurched out at him with his jaws open wide. There was the soundtrack's screech, followed by a gruesome snapping sound. Matt flinched because it felt for all the world like Springtrap was a split second away from biting his face off. Matt's avatar's corpse once again lay facedown (what was left of his face, anyway) in a fresh pool of blood. Springtrap grinned at his victory, his teeth stained red. He slowly licked the blood from his lips. The words GAME OVER *filled the screen again.*

Matt cursed, tore off his goggles, and threw them down on his desk. He should probably have been more careful with the expensive equipment, but he didn't care. Why did he keep losing to Springtrap? Why couldn't he win a game he had largely designed? He paced and cursed, then picked up a coffee mug and threw it. The mug smashed into tiny pieces and left a brown splatter on the clean white wall. *Good*, Matt thought. All of his thoughts were destructive.

There was a gentle knocking on the door, accompanied by the spoken words "Knock, knock." Why did people do that? Wasn't just knocking on the door enough?

"Yeah?" Matt snapped, not wanting to be bothered.

The door cracked and Jamie from the cubicle closest to his office peeked in. She was one of those women who looked like she hadn't changed her hair or clothing style since third grade. Her bangs were cut straight across her forehead, and she appeared to be wearing a jumper. "I heard noises and wanted to make sure you were okay."

"I'm fine. At least I was before you interrupted me," Matt snapped. Everybody in the office seemed to love Jamie. They raved about the homemade banana bread she'd leave in the break room and about how she was always willing to help out with a problem, whether professional or personal. But she didn't fool Matt. He knew Jamie was a busybody. It was like she was a vampire who fed on office drama.

"Sorry. I guess those were just the sounds of the creative process I was hearing?" Jamie quipped, crinkling her nose as she smiled. It was a cowering, ingratiating smile, like a dog wagging its tail when you had caught it peeing on the carpet.

"That's right," Matt said, not smiling back. What was he supposed to say—that he got mad because the big bunny had killed him twice in a row? That he had thrown his coffee mug against the wall because he couldn't handle the fact that he was losing to his own creation? Matt was starting to feel like the video game developer version of Dr. Frankenstein.

"Well, good luck. See you later," Jamie said, giving a little wave with just her fingers. "You want me to close the door back?"

"I never wanted you to open it in the first place."

He was going to go in again. This time he would make better choices. He would get past the murderous rabbit. He would lay to rest the nagging suspicion that this was a game he couldn't win.

Sometimes Matt felt like life was a game he couldn't win. Sure, he had all the trappings of a happy existence. He had graduated from a good school and married Hannah, his college sweetheart. He had gotten his dream job, and he and Hannah had bought a pretty four-bedroom house with ample room for her home office, his massive video game collection, and, Hannah had hoped, a growing family.

Back in college, Matt had enjoyed the excitement of pursuing and eventually winning Hannah. He had met her in a killer chemistry class freshman year, where she had an A average and he was struggling. He asked her to be his tutor, and they met twice a week. They worked on chemistry, but they also talked and laughed a lot. Finally, he had asked her, "Would you be willing to go out on a date with somebody who is way worse at chemistry than you?"

She said yes, and they soon were inseparable. Once they were really dating, she didn't even mind letting him copy down her problem sets. It gave them extra time to spend together doing other, more fun things. Their "meet cute" story was a big hit whenever people asked how they got together. They always said, "We had chemistry."

After graduation, Matt had loved going after and getting his dream job, hunting for and acquiring the right house. But once you won the prize, there was nothing to do but maintain it. And maintenance wasn't as interesting. The dream house had extensive plumbing problems, so many that it seemed like they should just ask a plumber to move into one of the extra bedrooms. The job was great sometimes, but there were also countless boring meetings during which people who knew much less than he did talked on and on about insignificant details, and he was expected to listen to them respectfully, which wasn't always possible. How could it be, when he clearly had the best ideas in the room?

And then there was the problem of maintaining a marriage. When they were dating, Matt had been so preoccupied with winning Hannah's love that he never thought about the cost of that prize, namely that he was committing to spending the rest of his life with one person and one person only. It had gotten boring quickly. The endless nights in, the same conversations about their days, the same chicken breasts and green salad for dinner and the same TV shows afterward. Hannah was still pretty and smart and nice, but the novelty had worn off her, like when you buy a new car and it's exciting at first but then it just settles in to being your car, reliable and useful but no longer a source of excitement.

There had been other problems as well. Hannah had wanted to start a family right away, and Matt hadn't. In fact, the more tedious the day-to-day grind of marriage had become, the less he had wanted to add kids to the equation. The whole prospect of parenting yawned before him as a string of unpleasant responsibilities stretching out for decades: the feedings and diaper changes and sleepless nights of infancy, the endless ferrying of school-age children to school and lessons and practices, the drama and rebellion of the teen years. All that, plus the stress of having to pay for college. Who needed it?

Apparently, Hannah had needed it. Or anyway, she had thought she did. Every Friday night when they would go out to the Neapolitan, their favorite Italian restaurant, she would wait until Matt had been softened up by a couple of glasses of wine and say, "I think it's time."

Matt would always say, "Time for dessert?" even though he knew good and well that tiramisu wasn't what she was talking about.

"Time to start a family," she would inevitably say.

He had tried to put her off in a variety of ways. He had said they still needed a few years to focus on their careers, but Hannah had said that since she ran her graphic design business from home, she could balance it with parenting now.

Once, Matt had suggested that, if she wanted something to take care of, they should get a dog instead of having a baby. That tactic hadn't gone over well.

The worst, though, was when he tried to argue that pregnancy and motherhood would ruin Hannah's petite, attractive figure. That time, she had called him shallow, thrown the contents of her water glass in his face, and stormed out of the restaurant.

The fact that Hannah wasn't willing to listen to reason about having a baby had definitely put a damper on their marriage. And then there was the matter of the harmless little friendship Matt had struck up with Brianna, a server at the restaurant where he frequently had lunch. It wasn't anything serious and it certainly wasn't any of Hannah's business, but she had gotten all upset when Matt had left his computer open and she saw that Brianna had sent him a picture of herself in a bikini. He had no idea why Hannah had been so unreasonable. Friends did that kind of thing all the time.

Hannah had suggested that the two of them get marriage counseling, but Matt had refused, and their marriage had ended in divorce shortly after their one-year anniversary. Since then, Matt had had a string of girlfriends, the first one being Brianna from the restaurant. None of these relationships had lasted over three months, and Matt was always the one who got dumped. This string of breakups was a major contributor to the rage Matt was able to summon in creating Springtrap.

Women were crazy, Matt had decided. And not worth the effort.

To combat his loneliness and frustration, Matt had thrown himself into the design of the VR game even more obsessively than usual. It was the cruelest of ironies that the game—much like his relationships—seemed to have turned against him.

But this time, he was going to outsmart the rabbit and get out of the maze alive.

Matt ran down the dark hallway and turned right into the room with the doors. He looked around and chose the door behind him. When he turned the knob and opened the door, the entrance was clear.

He walked down another dark hallway. There was no sign of Springtrap. He made a left into the hallway that led to a hall of mirrors. He knew his way through, of course. The trick was making sure he wasn't being followed. He moved his way past the panels of glass, each one identical. He was maybe twelve steps from the exit when he felt the presence of something behind him. In a mirror, he saw the reflection of the big green rabbit standing behind him. The rabbit grabbed him by the hair and raised a gleaming knife to Matt's throat.

Matt could almost feel the swift, sure slash.

Once again, Matt saw his avatar lying facedown, this time in a spreading puddle of his own blood. The rabbit licked the blood from the knife's blade and laughed, its shoulders shaking.

But it didn't feel like the rabbit was just laughing at Matt's mortally wounded avatar.

It felt like the rabbit was laughing at Matt himself.

So the rabbit wanted to play dirty, did it? Matt yanked off his headpiece. He reached out his arms and cleared his desk, sending all its contents clattering to the floor. He would show that rabbit who was in charge; he just needed some room to spread out. He was in control of the game, so he was in control of the rabbit. He got to say what it could and could not do, where it could and could not go. He would show it who was boss. When Matt went home later, he wouldn't have that much control over his life, but here, inside the game, he was the absolute ruler, and all of the decisions were his to make.

He programmed the game such that Springtrap was doomed to wander the maze alone all night, with no victims to stalk and no way out. He also sped up the game's time frame by one thousand, so that for each minute that passed in real time, one thousand minutes passed for Springtrap. Matt found himself laughing louder and harder than he had laughed in a long time. Sure, the rabbit might be able to kill his avatar, but that was nothing compared to the way that Matt could alter Springtrap's reality, could control time and space and mete out a cosmic punishment like some kind of ancient, vengeful god.

Matt left the office and laughed some more on the drive home.

Hannah had gotten the house in the divorce, so Matt had moved into one of those apartment complexes with a pool and tennis courts, which advertised itself as offering "affordable luxury." He had furnished the apartment with simple, functional pieces and lots of shelving for his video game collection. When his friend Jason from college had gotten kicked to the curb by his girlfriend at the same time one of Matt's three-month relationships had split up, Matt had invited him to move into the extra bedroom and split the rent.

When Matt walked into the apartment, Jason was sitting on the couch in front of the big-screen TV with a video game controller in hand. It wasn't even six o'clock, and he had already changed into his pajamas. A two-liter bottle of soda and an open bag of cheese puffs decorated the coffee table. "Hey," he said, not looking away from the zombies he was blasting on the screen.

"Hey," Matt said.

"And how is Springtrap?" Jason asked, like one might ask about a friend's sick aunt.

Matt smiled. "Springtrap is going to have an interesting evening."

"Wait, what?" Jason said.

"Nothing." Matt tossed his bag on the couch. "The game is going great. Kids are going to love it."

"Big kids, too," Jason said. "I can't wait to play it myself. Hey, what do you want for dinner tonight? Pizza? Thai? Chinese?" He nodded toward the stack of takeout menus on the coffee table.

Matt shrugged. "Whatever. You pick. I'm going to take a quick shower." He had gotten all sweaty and agitated during his battle with the rabbit earlier, but now he could relax and have his revenge at the same time, knowing that the helpless creature was doomed to wander aimlessly through the maze all night.

Matt and Jason ate their Thai takeout straight from the containers while sitting on the couch and watching an episode of *Reign of Stones* Jason had recorded on the DVR. Living with Jason felt like being in college all over again. At first it had been fun—no complicated female emotions, no home repairs, no yard to mow. After work, it was all takeout and TV and video games unless one of them had a date.

But lately the carefree college vibe had started to wear thin, and Matt had begun to feel like he was regressing, losing ground at a time in life when he should be gaining. Plus, Jason had started to get on his nerves. He was so unambitious, working at a dead-end call center job and never looking for anything more lucrative or challenging. How could a person be so *chill* all the time? Before long, Matt was going to have to make some decisions about how to move forward with his life.

As the episode of *Reign of Stones* grew more violent, Matt's thoughts turned to Springtrap in the VR game, wandering endlessly, aimlessly, with nowhere to go and no one to kill. Matt smiled. It served the psychotic bunny right for killing him all those times.

It was strange that thinking about the trapped Springtrap made Matt feel a little better. Maybe he couldn't control the people around him, but he was in charge when it came to the game. If he didn't like the way things were going, he just had to do a little bit of programming to change the outcome.

After a mostly sleepless night, Matt was happy to be back at work, where at least things were interesting some of the time. In the break area, he helped himself to a cup of coffee he knew would be bad, then made his way to his office to see how Springtrap's night had been. At least Matt knew that there was somebody who had had a worse night than his.

Matt put on his headset and entered the game. He walked down the dim hallway and turned right to arrive at the room with the doors. He chose the door on the right. Thankfully, Springtrap wasn't there, so he was granted access to the rest of the maze. Matt walked around the maze for a long time, but there was no sign of Springtrap. No jump scares, no sneaking up behind him, no quick glimpses of the rabbit at the end of a hall.

It was strange. The way the game was programmed, he should have seen Springtrap by now.

Matt took off his headset and opened the game's data log. For several in-game days, Springtrap had wandered around the perimeters of the maze, looking for someone to kill. This was what Matt had expected.

But he hadn't expected what he saw next.

After all those days with no one to kill when killing was his life's only purpose, Springtrap seemed to spawn a new version of himself. Immediately, the new version killed the old version. And then the current Springtrap would somehow produce a newer version, which would then kill it.

The cycle went on and on: creation of a new AI, followed by the newly created one destroying the creator. The killings got faster and faster, one right after another, seemingly as soon as the newest Springtrap was able to spawn an even newer model. The murders grew in violence just as they grew in speed. Stabbings, slashings, decapitations. When Matt saw the word *disembowelment* in the data log, he felt the coffee lurch in his stomach.

While bizarre, the log did at least answer the question of how Springtrap had spent the night. What it didn't answer was where Springtrap was now.

The rabbit was programmed into the game's code. He didn't have the ability to truly, permanently kill himself. He would always respawn. He had to be in there somewhere.

Matt searched the game's VR for Springtrap. He searched parts of the game where Springtrap wasn't even programmed to be. After having spawned and killed half a million versions of himself over the course of the night, the rabbit seemed to have disappeared.

Except that he *couldn't* really disappear. It wasn't possible.

The code. The answer had to be in the code.

Matt could be absentminded sometimes. Hannah used to tease him about his endless ability to lose his car keys or his cell phone, but he had an amazing memory when it came to programming. As a result, it was shocking when he looked at the program for Springtrap and saw that it now bore absolutely no resemblance to the program he had created. Springtrap's programming was fractured, splintered, unrecognizable. He had no choice but to remove it and start over.

He went through the usual steps to remove it, but the damaged program remained.

He figured that, since he was tired, he might have entered something incorrectly. He tried again, but the results were the same. He tried again and again for an hour. Two hours. Three. But the results never varied. The damaged program could not be removed.

It was as if Springtrap, in one last spectacular suicide, had blown himself to smithereens, and now all those tiny bits of him were scattered throughout the game's code, as impossible to retrieve as individual specks of dust.

Matt started to sweat. All over the internet and in every game store, ads for the new *Five Nights at Freddy's* virtual reality game abounded, announcing a release date that was all too soon. And now the game's program was defective in a way that apparently could not be fixed? Matt's revenge on Springtrap seemed ridiculously small compared to Springtrap's revenge on him.

Maybe if he went into the game one more time, he could figure out some way to reverse the damage.

Matt's avatar ran around the periphery of the maze looking for signs of Springtrap. He turned a corner and caught sight of something green up ahead.

Springtrap's lifeless body lay around the maze's next bend. It was splayed on its back with its torso split wide open. Matt kneeled for a closer look. Springs and gears protruded from the edge of the gaping wound. How could something so mechanical manage to look so dead? Springtrap's blank, sightless stare was horrible to behold. Matt reached up to the rabbit's eyelids to close them.

As soon as he made physical contact, Matt felt a sharp sting combined with a mild electrical jolt that reminded him of the pain of getting his fraternity letters tattooed on his ankle in college. He pulled the avatar's hand away.

Matt was too stressed out about the strange state of the game to be in the mood for a date, but Jason had been insistent. The girl Jason was dating had promised him that her roommate would be perfect for Matt. The four of them were supposed to have dinner together at the Neapolitan, Hannah and Matt's old go-to Italian restaurant. This was another reason Matt didn't want to go—too many memories, both good and bad. But the main reason was that he thought the likelihood of this girl being perfect for him was equivalent to the likelihood of a snowstorm in August.

When the doorbell rang, Matt answered to find two young women, one of them blonde and athletically pretty with a sun-kissed complexion. Maybe this evening would be better than he predicted.

"Well, hello," Matt said to her, turning on his most charming smile. "This is a pleasant surprise. Usually, I think Jason's kind of an idiot, but when he said we'd be perfect for each other, he definitely knew what he was talking about." He held out his hand.

The pretty blonde didn't take his proffered hand and only gave him a small smile back. "I'm Meghan, Jason's date. This is your date, Eva." She gestured toward the brown-haired young woman Matt hadn't even noticed standing beside her.

"Hi," Eva said, smiling shyly. She was dressed in a striped button-down blouse and khakis, like she was going to work instead of on a date.

"Hi," Matt said, not bothering to hide his disappointment. Eva wasn't ugly, exactly. It was just that, standing beside a specimen as fine as Meghan, she looked like a sparrow next to a bird of paradise. Matt also noticed that Eva's smile had not benefited from orthodontia. *Her parents must have been too poor to pay for braces*, he figured. Matt always found that the state of a person's teeth was an accurate indicator of social class. So were shoes. He glanced down at Eva's footwear. Cheap flats.

"So are we allowed to come in?" Meghan asked.

"Of course," Matt said, stepping aside. "Hey, Jason!" he called. "The ladies are here."

Jason stumbled into the living room, his hair still wet from the shower. He came up to Meghan and kissed her cheek, then said, "Hey, Eva, have you met Matt?"

"Yes, we've met," she said. Matt couldn't figure out why she didn't sound more enthusiastic. She was lucky to be going on this date. A guy like him would usually be way out of her league. And speaking of being out of one's league, how did a schlubby guy like Jason get a shot with a gorgeous girl like Meghan?

"Hey," Jason said, "I thought we could take separate cars to the restaurant. That way if we want to do anything separately after dinner, we're all set."

"Fine with me," Matt said. Taking his own car would give him the ability to cut the evening short if it proved too unbearable.

Matt saw Jason open his car door for Meghan, so he bit the bullet and did the same for Eva. Of course, Jason's car was the same one he'd been driving since college, and Matt's was a new sports car. He was surprised that Eva didn't compliment him on it.

On the way to the restaurant, Eva said, "So Jason tells me you're a video game developer. That's really cool."

"Yeah," Matt said, trying to not think about the disappeared code that was endangering his high-profile project. "It is really cool. Right now I'm working on the newest *Five Nights at Freddy's* game, the VR one. It's going great," he said, trying to convince himself at least as much as he was trying to convince her.

"My little brother is dying to get that game as soon as it comes out," Eva said. "It's practically all he talks about. He won't believe that I know the developer."

Well, now she was showing some enthusiasm at least. Matt decided to lob the ball into her court. "So what is it that you do?" He wasn't particularly interested, but he told himself to try to listen to her answer.

"I'm in the IT department at the recreational outfitting company where Meghan works," she said. "That's one of the reasons Jason thought you and I might get along, because we're both into tech stuff."

"Yeah, well, the last thing I want to talk about once I get home from work is 'tech stuff,'" Matt said.

Eva's smile looked forced. "Yeah, me too."

They didn't talk about anything else for the rest of the drive to the restaurant.

Matt hadn't been to the Neapolitan since the divorce. It was the same as it had always been, dimly lit and romantic with violin music playing softly in the background. The elderly maître d' looked at him with a glow of recognition. "Oh, I remember you!" he said. "You used to come here all the time with your lovely wife."

"Well, she's not my lovely wife anymore," Matt grumbled. Why couldn't people mind their own business?

The maître d' blanched but quickly regained his composure. "Oh, I see. Table for four, then?"

Matt ordered the osso bucco, his favorite. Meghan ordered the same, which Matt felt indicated discerning taste. Both Jason and Eva ordered the spaghetti with meat sauce. Matt was appalled by their lack of sophistication. They might as well have ordered from the children's menu.

It was then that an idea began to form in Matt's mind. Weren't he and Meghan much more compatible than Jason and Meghan? After all, Matt and Meghan were both attractive, sophisticated people. Jason and Eva, though . . . they were both *nice* for what that was worth, but they lacked looks, drive, and sophistication. They were spaghetti with meat sauce to Matt and Meghan's osso bucco.

What if Matt could use this date as an opportunity to charm Meghan away from Jason? Meghan was clearly more compatible with Matt, and maybe there would be no hard feelings since Jason could have Eva as a consolation prize. Plus, maybe getting his love life in order might give Matt the peace he needed to figure out whatever the problem in the game was and fix it once and for all.

When the waiter came with their salads, Matt said, "I think we'd like to get a bottle of pinot grigio for the table."

"Very good, sir," the waiter said.

"Thanks, man," Jason said. "Big spender."

Matt shrugged. "You can't be stingy if you're going to have a good time. It takes money to have good food, good wine, good friends."

"It doesn't take money to have good friends," Eva said.

So what—she was going to pick an argument with him? "Well, it takes money to have a good time with your friends. How about that?" Matt said.

"Not really," Eva said, pushing her salad around her plate. "Some of the best times I've ever had with my friends have been just hanging out and talking."

"Yes, but good food and good wine certainly enhance

conversation," Matt said. "What do you think, Meghan?"

"Well, they can," Meghan said. "But I agree with Eva. Sometimes the best times are just hanging out in your pajamas talking all night and eating peanut butter out of the jar."

Matt figured Meghan didn't want to make her friend feel bad.

When the wine arrived, Matt offered to pour some for Eva, but she put her hand over the glass and said, "No thank you. I don't drink."

Well, she's no fun, Matt thought. He poured wine for Jason and then poured Meghan's glass extra full. The more she drank, the more charming she would find him.

Over dinner, Matt told interesting stories about his life and accomplishments. Sure, he may have felt a little guilty that he didn't let Jason get a word in edgewise, but it was important that Meghan get to know the kind of guy he was.

Between the entrées and the tiramisu, Jason and Eva both excused themselves to go to the restroom, leaving Matt at the table alone with Meghan. The opportunity couldn't have been more perfect.

"So, I know you've got this thing going with Jason now because . . . well, opposites attract, I guess," Matt said, smiling at her. The candlelight shined on her golden hair. She really was lovely. "But I just want to say that I find you devastatingly attractive, and I'd like to give you my number. Just in case you'd like it for, you know, future reference."

Meghan's blue eyes flashed. "I thought you and Jason were best friends."

Matt was surprised to hear the anger in her voice. "Well, we are, but you know what they say, 'All's fair in love and war.'"

"Just because 'they' say it doesn't mean it's true," Meghan said. "All evening you've talked about nothing but yourself and how great you supposedly are. Maybe Jason isn't as well dressed as you and doesn't have as impressive a job as you, but he's great because he's a nice, caring guy."

Matt wasn't going to sit there and take this abuse from yet another delusional woman. "Well, I hope you enjoy your life of poverty with your nice, caring guy," he said, getting up from the table. He was so angry he felt smoke might come out of his ears, as though he were a character in an old cartoon. "This evening has been an utter disaster. I trust that you and Jason will be nice enough to give my alleged 'date,' what's-her-name, a ride." He grabbed the wine bottle and marched out of the restaurant.

It was only when he was in the car that he realized he had left without paying his part of the bill. *Good*, he thought. *Let them take care of it.* It served them right for not appreciating him.

He drove home too fast, thinking of what a wretched day it had been. It felt like the problems with the game had infected his whole life. But that was going to change.

★ ★ ★

Matt woke up feeling strangely queasy. Usually morning tummy trouble was a symptom of his having drunk too much the night before. He had polished off that bottle of wine last night, but still, it hadn't added up to more than three glasses' worth. He shouldn't be hung over.

Coffee, he decided, was the solution, as it was to many of life's problems. He dragged himself into the kitchen and put on a pot to brew. Though the thought of eating was unpleasant, he dropped a slice of whole wheat bread into the toaster in case his stomach's emptiness was the cause of its unrest.

Once the brewing and toasting were complete, he sat down at the kitchen table. One sip of coffee and one bite of toast later, his stomach roiled violently. Without even having made a conscious decision to move, he found himself leaning over the kitchen sink, retching up not only the toast and coffee but seemingly everything else he had consumed over the past few days.

He rinsed out the sink, wet a paper towel, and used it to dab his sweaty forehead. His body couldn't have chosen a worse time to get sick. He couldn't miss work. He had to fix the game.

He would fix it by lunchtime, he decided. Then he could take the rest of the day off to rest and recover.

It was almost noon, and Matt's stomach was still roiling like a storm at sea. He had moved the wastebasket next to his desk so he could hurl into it as needed. Eating lunch was unimaginable.

He had been working nonstop to repair the game with no success. He had consulted every manual he owned. He had read extensively from a variety of specialized sites on the internet. He had even put in a phone call to one of his old professors from grad school, but it was all to no avail.

Matt wasn't used to feeling stupid or like a failure, but now he was experiencing both of these unpleasant, unaccustomed feelings. It was like Springtrap, his own creation, had bested him.

There was a knock on his office door. "Come in," Matt said. He hoped it was either someone to save him or someone to put him out of his misery.

"Hiya, Matt." It was neither. It was Gary, the head of his department, who was guaranteed in any given situation to (a) be of no help whatsoever, and (b) deepen his misery. Matt gritted his teeth.

"Hey, Gary." Matt hoped the signs of his distress weren't visible, but he was pretty sure they were. He was breathing heavily and sweating like he'd just run a marathon. The intensity of his nausea made it difficult to speak. He was afraid that if he opened his mouth, something other than words would come out.

Gary sat down in the chair across from Matt's desk. He was, as always, impeccably groomed—his hair in a perfect, Ken-doll part, his expensive suit wrinkle free. "Have you been on social media the past couple of days?" He grinned, flashing his perfectly straight, white teeth. "Kids are going nuts over this game—some adults, too. It's gonna be huge, Matt. *Huge.*"

"Huge," Matt echoed, trying to smile but failing. His mouth refused to go up at the corners.

"So how's it going?" Gary asked, leaning forward in his chair. "Is everything moving forward like it needs to? Because I tell you, that deadline is *looming.*"

Matt didn't need to be told that the deadline was looming. "It's going great," he said, hoping he sounded more convincing than he felt.

"Good to hear," Gary said, like he was trying to decide whether he believed him. "Anything I can help you with?"

"No, it's going great," Matt repeated, his voice getting a little high-pitched and whiny the way it did when he was nervous.

"Excellent!" Gary said, getting up from the chair. "Can't wait to see what you've put together. You'll be ready to present it on Friday, right?"

"Friday. You bet," Matt said, gulping.

Gary left, closing the door behind him. Matt put his head down on his desk in despair. He had started the morning feeling confident in his ability to solve the problem, but the skies had darkened.

Matt took his lunch break, not to eat, but just to get out of the office and try to clear his head. He walked the half block to Gus's, a dimly lit dive bar that reminded him of the cheap places he used to frequent in college. Maybe he could just sip on a soda to settle his stomach. Also,

Gus's wouldn't be crowded at lunchtime, and maybe the combination of a soda and the dark and the quiet would help him think.

Matt placed his order, and Gus filled it. Matt wished that all relationships could be that simple. He sipped his cola and thought. Okay, so there was no time for a major redesign, but was there anything else he could do that might save the game and save his job?

Matt looked around the room. In the corner were a couple of old video game cabinets that had probably been there since the games were new in the eighties. He stared at the demo screen of an old maze game, watching a weird yellow ball guy being pursued by candy-colored ghosts. Then the thought hit him.

I can just program in a new Springtrap, one that follows the path it's supposed to. The old program is so messed up it won't have any impact on the game anyway. No one will even know it's there.

Why hadn't he thought of this before? The problem was as good as solved. He ate a handful of bar peanuts and finished his soda. Something about the combination of saltiness and fizziness soothed his stomach. Then he went back to the office to build a new Springtrap, one that followed the path it was supposed to follow.

And this time, Matt wouldn't antagonize the rabbit. He had learned his lesson.

It hadn't been easy hacking into the company's computer, but Gene had done it. Maybe it was a sign that things were looking up. Life hadn't been going great for him lately. He had gotten fired from his job on the Nerd Team at Good Deal electronics store and had had to move back in with his parents until he could find something else, which hadn't happened yet. It was depressing being a grown man living in your childhood bedroom, looking at all those old trophies from Scholar's Bowl and math team and realizing how little they meant.

That was why he'd been packing on the weight. Depression and Mom's home cooking were a dangerous combination.

But now he at least had one thing going for him. He had his own early copy of *Springtrap's Revenge*. Because of his superior hacking skills, he was going to be one of the first people—if not the very first person—to play the game. And with his superior gaming skills, he might very well become the very first person to beat the game, too. And that would be an accomplishment.

He put on the VR headset. He was ready to play.

Gene created an avatar that looked like his ideal self, like he would look again once he got back on his feet. Getting into the computer system and getting this game was a good sign, Gene thought. A success that would be the first in a series of successes.

Once his avatar was created, Gene found himself standing at the end of a dark hallway. He walked to the opposite end. There was a door on the left and a door on the right. Randomly, he chose the one on the right. He found himself in a room with four doors.

Clearly, he had to choose one, and from his past experiences with FNAF games, he knew that the wrong choice would result in a jump scare and a GAME OVER *screen.*

He chose the door on the left. He took a deep breath, turned the knob, and pulled. It was clear. He breathed a sigh of relief, took a few steps forward, and found himself in another dark hallway. He walked forward until he slammed into a wall. He had to say, the VR features were impressive. When his avatar hit the wall, he could feel the bump.

He felt his way to the right, where there was a passage forward, and continued feeling his way along the wall. Between the limited perspective offered by the VR and the lack of light, this maze was obviously no joke. But if there was one area in his life where Gene had full confidence in himself, it was gaming. He was going to find his way out.

It was strange. It seemed like part of the fun of negotiating the maze should be avoiding creepy characters who lurked around corners and jumped out when least expected. But so far, there were no creepy characters in sight, not even the title character. The game was called Springtrap's Revenge. *So where was Springtrap?*

"Gene Junior! Dinner's ready!" a voice called from the kitchen, breaking Gene's immersion in the game. "Stuffed peppers and macaroni and cheese!"

"I'll be there in a minute, Ma!" Gene yelled back. But he knew it would be longer than a minute. He wasn't leaving the game until he found Springtrap.

Besides, if there was one thing he knew about Ma, it

was that she wasn't going to let him go hungry. If he took too long to come to the table, she'd make him a plate and bring it to his room, so he could shovel in his dinner while he played.

Gene saw something green sticking out from behind a corner of the maze. He went to investigate, steeling himself for a jump scare, but the version of Springtrap he found, while undoubtedly scary, was incapable of jumping out at anyone.

Springtrap's body lay motionless and flat on its back, its abdomen flayed open. Springs and gears protruded from the wound. Its eyes were open and empty.

Gene thought it might be a trick, that any second the green rabbit would spring to life and grab Gene's avatar's ankle. But the rabbit just lay there. Gene made his avatar nudge it with his foot, but it was inert. It seemed to be GAME OVER *for Springtrap.*

But that didn't make any sense. If this game was about Springtrap getting revenge, why would the supposed main character be dead in the beginning? Unless the plot turned into some kind of ghost story?

"Gene Junior! Your dinner's getting cold!"

"I'll be there in a minute, Ma! Just let me finish . . . filling out this job application," Gene called. He knew if she thought he was applying for a job, she'd stay off his back for a few more minutes.

He had to figure out what was going on in *Springtrap's Revenge,* and the only way to do it was to take a look at the code. It was time to put those superior hacking skills to use again.

After a few commands, he was in. But what he found made no sense. According to the code, Springtrap had been extracted from the very game that bore his name in the title. The program that initiated the extraction was inexplicably called "Its_a_boy.exe."

Matt was hungry. Ravenous. He was sitting at a table for two at Ye Olde Steakhouse. His companion at the table was Madison, who, thankfully, was as pretty as her pictures, with shiny chestnut hair and big, doelike brown eyes.

This was their first date, but Matt was having a hard time focusing on the required chitchat because he was so hungry. He realized he had scooted the breadbasket in front of him and had been mindlessly gnawing his way through the rolls. "I'm sorry. Would you like some bread?" he asked, forcing himself to push the basket in her direction.

"No thanks," she said with an awkward grin. "I'm watching my carbs."

"Not me, obviously," Matt said, trying for humor as he tore off another chunk of bread with his teeth. What was this? Roll number four? Number five?

The server appeared, and before she could even ask them for their order, Matt said, "Porterhouse steak, very rare, with a loaded baked potato and creamed spinach on the side. And let's get a refill on this breadbasket, too."

"And for you, ma'am?" The server turned to Madison. Matt figured this was a subtle jab at him, a reminder that he was supposed to have let the lady order first, but he was far too hungry to care about etiquette. He was so hungry that it felt like a medical emergency.

"The Cobb salad, please, with blue cheese dressing on the side," Madison said.

Matt hoped the server would hurry back with that new breadbasket before he started trying to eat the tablecloth. "You know, I've always wondered," he said, "you girls always order salads when you're out on dates . . . like you don't want a guy seeing you eat too much. When you go out with your girlfriends, do you order something else? Like a big plate of ribs or something?"

Ribs, Matt thought. *Ribs sound delicious.*

Madison smiled. "It depends on how hungry I am. Sometimes when I go out with my best friend, we split a burger and fries."

"You *split* a burger and fries?" Matt said. "That's just like an appetizer or something."

Madison giggled. "It's really not. Half a cheeseburger is plenty. And girls can't eat like you guys can. If I look at a piece of cheesecake, I gain five pounds."

Cheesecake. For dessert, Matt definitely wanted cheesecake. He rarely ordered dessert, but he was going for it tonight. *Stop*, he told himself. *Stop obsessing over food, and notice your date.* "Well," he said finally, "whatever you're doing, you should keep on doing it because you look fantastic."

"Thanks," she said, smiling.

Good, Matt thought. *When in doubt, give a compliment. It always smooths things over.*

When the food arrived, Matt felt like a starving lumberjack. The rare steak sat in an appetizing pool of blood, and when Matt cut into it, the meat was a purply red.

"I think I just heard it moo," Madison said as Matt held a dripping chunk of meat to his lips.

"Well, you won't hear it long because it's going to be in my belly," Matt said. The nearly raw meat was delicious, so intensely so that Matt closed his eyes as he chewed. He ignored the vegetables on his plate and sawed into the meat over and over again, cutting off big chunks that filled his cheeks as he chewed. He resented how the knife and fork slowed down his eating. Really, it would make much more sense just to pick up the steak and rend off chunks with his canines. That's what they were for, weren't they?

Table manners, all the rules of etiquette, really, were just ways to delay the body getting what it needed. And Matt's body needed this meat.

He wasn't quite sure when he had picked up the large T-bone from the center of the steak and started gnawing it, growling to himself with animal pleasure.

But then he felt Madison's eyes on him. She was sitting across from him, holding a forkful of lettuce in midair, staring at him like he was an exhibit in a zoo.

Then he felt the eyes of the other customers at the other tables as well.

He set down the bone. "I went to the doctor the other day," he lied. "He said I was terribly anemic. I must have needed this red meat something fierce."

"You must have," Madison said. She reached into her handbag, pulled out her phone, and looked at it for a second. "Oh no," she said. "I just got a text from my roommate. My cat is sick. I have to go. Thanks for dinner."

She didn't stick around long enough to hear Matt say, "I'll call you."

Why couldn't he satisfy this bottomless hunger? His steak was gone now, and so were the baked potato and creamed spinach. He reached across the table for the rest of Madison's mostly uneaten salad. It would be a shame for it to go to waste.

As Matt got undressed for his bedtime shower, he caught a glimpse of his reflection in the bathroom mirror and almost didn't recognize himself. His belly was definitely bigger. He was bloated from the enormous dinner he had eaten at the steakhouse, but this seemed like more than standard post-meal bloat. Matt looked at his handsome face and shrugged. What were a few more pounds? He was still looking good. And historically, being a man with a little extra weight was a sign of prosperity.

Matt woke up with a goal that was crystal clear in its simplicity: to make it to the bathroom before it was too late. He threw off the covers and ran, then spewed the remains of last night's huge and expensive dinner into the porcelain bowl. He retched and gagged long after there was nothing left to bring up.

Strangely, he still felt bloated afterward, and his belly was still distended. Was this some kind of weird virus, the symptoms of which were cycles of extreme nausea followed by extreme hunger? If it was a virus, it was certainly hanging on a long time. He would have to ask people at work if they had heard of anybody else having the same symptoms.

"Matt, are you feeling okay?" Jamie asked as they sat in the conference room waiting for a meeting to start. Her brow was knitted in a look of concern, but Matt doubted that it was genuine.

"Oh, it's just this bug I'm having a hard time fighting off," Matt said. The smell of the coffee in the room, usually one of his favorite aromas, was nauseating. "I'm either nauseated or starving, and I'm bloated and gassy. Do you know about any viruses with those symptoms going around?"

"I don't," Jamie said. "And I know about all the bugs because I have kids in school who bring them home!" She smiled. "Seriously, though, maybe you should have a doctor check you out. You're definitely bloated, and your color doesn't look good—you're kind of yellowish, like you might have jaundice. Maybe you should get some blood work done and get your liver function checked just to be on the safe side."

"Oh, doctors don't know anything," Matt said. And neither did Jamie. He didn't even know why he had bothered to ask her anything.

Gary walked in, which had the negative effect of starting the meeting but the positive effect of ending any other conversation.

"Good morning," Gary said, taking his place at the head of the conference table. "Well, the release date is in two weeks, and the reviews from early screening copies of the game are in. And the results are"—he looked down at his notes—"mixed."

Jamie let out a little sigh.

"According to the reviewers," Gary said, "the story line is good, the game play is challenging, and the number of jump scares is consistent with what *FNAF* fans expect." He cleared his throat. "*However*, every single reviewer agreed on one fact: the AI design of Springtrap is sloppy and not up to the game's usual standards."

Gary didn't call out Matt by name, but he might as well have. With Springtrap's bizarre series of regenerations and deaths after Matt had left him to wander the maze, Matt had really needed to rush to create a new AI to plug into the game. But he had been confident that despite the last-minute nature of the work, he had still done a good job. Well, good enough, anyway.

"Oh, is that what *reviewers* are saying?" Matt said. His face heated up with anger. "Are you going to tell me who these people are, or are they really just you?"

"Hey, hey," Gary said, holding his hands up as if defending himself. "No need to get all riled up. I'm just saying that in this competitive climate, nobody can afford to be doing anything but their best work."

"I always do my best work!" Matt said, raising his voice. "In fact, I would be doing some of it right now if you weren't wasting my time in this pointless meeting."

Jamie reached out to touch Matt's arm, but he jerked it away.

"I know these meetings take away time that you would use to work and think," Gary said. "And I promise this one won't last long. But after the meeting, Matt, as you are working and thinking, I would suggest that one of the things you should think about is the appropriate way to talk to your supervisor."

Matt drove home in a rage. He broke the speed limit by double digits and powered through red lights. *Let a cop pull me over*, he thought. *Just let him.*

Both anger and hunger were gnawing at him, even though he was so bloated and gassy that it felt like a pinprick to his stomach would cause it to pop like a balloon. When he drove by a burger joint, the smell of hot grease lured him to turn in. He went through the drive-thru and ordered a double bacon cheeseburger, large fries, and a chocolate shake—food that he would generally dismiss as too unhealthy for human consumption. Not wanting to have to slow down his eating because he was also driving, he pulled into a parking space and devoured the greasy meat and carbs like a ravenous wolverine.

His hunger subsided some. His anger did not.

When he got to the apartment, Jason was packing video games from his shelf into a cardboard box. Other filled boxes were scattered across the floor.

"What's going on?" Matt asked, though he had a feeling he knew.

"Listen, man," Jason said, not looking up at him, "Meghan finally told me what you did. She said she almost didn't because we're roommates, but then she decided that I needed to know. She said you hit on her when you were supposed to be getting to know Eva. You gave her your number when you knew she was on a date with me. Not cool, man."

"Okay," Matt said, "if you want me to apologize, I'll apologize." He didn't see the need for an apology, though. He hadn't been trying to forcibly take Meghan away from Jason. He had just been presenting her with choices.

Jason shook his head. "See, that's just it. I don't want you to apologize. I want you to stop being a jerk. But unfortunately, I don't see that ever happening. So I'm moving out. You spent our whole meal the other night talking about how prosperous and successful you are . . . right before you left us with the bill. You don't need my help with the rent. You can afford this place without me."

"I can," Matt said. "But I want you to stay." He didn't know why, but he had a sudden, desperate need not to be alone. It was a vague but persistent feeling that if he were left alone, something bad would happen.

"Yeah, and Eva wanted you to be nice to her, but she didn't get that wish, either. She's a super nice person, Matt. She deserved better."

"Yeah, you fixed me up with the girl with 'the great personality,'" Matt said, laughing bitterly. "You kept the pretty one for yourself."

Jason threw up his hands. "Okay, look. I can't have this conversation right now. I'm leaving. Tonight I'm borrowing a truck from a buddy. I'll come back in the morning and get my stuff when you're at work. I think it's best if you and I stay out of each other's way for a while."

Jason grabbed his keys and was out the door.

Matt got a beer from the fridge and sat down on the couch. How had things gotten so bad so fast? He didn't really need to ask. He knew the answer.

It was the rabbit. He couldn't explain it, but somehow the rabbit was to blame.

The beer tasted sour and unpleasant, and Matt felt the sickly blooming of a headache above his right temple. He reached up to massage his head and felt a hard knob pushing against his scalp. Was it possible he had gotten hit in the head hard enough for a knot to form and didn't remember it? And if he didn't remember it, what did that mean—that he had some kind of brain injury that was causing him to lose his mind? Or maybe it was his physical health, not his mental health, he should be worried about.

Matt needed someone to talk to about his problems, but there was no one. Hannah had abandoned him. A string of ungrateful girlfriends had abandoned him. And now Jason, his best friend, had abandoned him. As if that weren't all bad enough, he was unappreciated and criticized at work.

Perhaps such loneliness was the sad price to pay for his brilliance. Like so many geniuses before him, he was isolated and misunderstood. For the first time in his adult life, Matt found himself crying real tears.

Matt couldn't fasten his pants. Yesterday, they had been a tight fit but still a fit, but today they were impossible. Today he had lounged around in pajama pants all day, but now, trying to fit into real pants, it was apparent that his belly had swollen such that his size 34 waistline was only a fond memory. He tried another, more forgiving pair and then another, all to no avail. The discarded pants lay strewn on his bed.

The problem was that he had a date in a few minutes, and while he did find most rules of etiquette to be stupid and oppressive, he did accept the fact that a public date generally required one to wear pants. He dug through his closet and found a size 36 in the very back. He stepped into them, but they still wouldn't fasten over his belly. Finally, he pulled them down below the mountainous swelling and managed to zip them up. The button still wouldn't close, but he managed to secure them with a belt. It wasn't the ideal situation, but it would have to do.

Matt had arranged to meet his new date, another internet acquaintance, in a bar. This way, he reasoned, if the date turned out to be as disastrous as his last ones, at least he wouldn't have to pay for dinner.

The bar was one of those sleek, modern places favored by young urban professionals, all chrome and glass and indirect lighting. Walking in, he caught his reflection in one of the place's many mirrors and was momentarily startled. His belly was so bloated that the buttons of his shirt were straining, the gaps between the buttons revealing his yellowish skin. His face and hair were drenched in sweat. And was it his imagination, or was his hair also getting thinner?

Still, Matt knew he had a lot more going for him than any of the losers in this bar. Emma—that was the new girl's name, right?—Emma was lucky to be going out with him.

He didn't recognize her at first. She was sitting at a table alone and gave him a little wave. Her face was pretty like he remembered it being on the dating site, and so was her honey-blonde hair. But the picture she used on the site must have been taken a good twenty-five pounds ago. The girl was *chunky*. It was a good thing he hadn't committed to taking her out to dinner. He probably couldn't afford to feed her.

Well, it was too late to slip out now. She had already spotted him. He pasted on a smile and walked up to the table. "Emma?"

"Matt!" She smiled broadly and gestured for him to sit down.

"So what are we drinking?"

"Hmm . . . appletini?"

"One fruity girl drink coming up. Let me go converse with the barkeep." He went to the bar and ordered the Girl Drink for Emma and a martini for himself. It was strong, but he had a feeling he was going to need it to get through this date.

"Yum, thank you," Emma said when he set down the toxic-looking green drink in front of her. "Thanks for picking out this place. It's really cool. I'm ashamed to admit I don't get out much. Most nights after work I just put on my pajamas and watch Netflix."

And eat a gallon of ice cream, Matt thought, but he just smiled and nodded. "Yeah, sometimes I just end up hanging out with my roommate and playing video games," Matt said. Then he remembered Jason wasn't his roommate anymore. No need to tell her that, though. He had already decided he was never going to see her again.

"Well, you're a video game developer," she said, sipping her cocktail, "so when you hang out and play video games that's like research, right?"

He managed a strained smile. Something was happening in his abdomen. Pressure was building in an unpleasant way, almost like a force was pushing his belly from the inside. He took a sip of his martini, which hit his stomach like battery acid. He must have grimaced because Emma asked, "Are you okay?"

"Sure, sure," he said. But he wasn't. He felt like he was

going to burst like an overripe berry. He couldn't sit here and make polite chitchat. "But let me just go ahead and tell you right now that this isn't going to work out. So you enjoy your drink, and I'm going to say good night."

"Now wait just a second," Emma said. "You've barely even talked to me. It's way too soon to figure out whether you think I'm an interesting person or not. So tell me, how do you know this isn't going to work out?"

Was she going to force him to say it? Apparently she was. "Okay, Emma, I'm sure you have a great personality. But when you post a picture of yourself on a dating site, it needs to look like you, not you twenty-five pounds ago."

Emma's mouth dropped open. "I can't believe you have the nerve to say that to me! First of all, it's shallow and offensive. But second of all, have you looked in a mirror lately? Feel free. They're everywhere in this place. Your picture online is at least thirty-five pounds ago! Did I notice that when you came in? Sure. But it didn't bother me. What *does* bother me is that you're a gigantic hypocrite!"

"Fine. Well, I think the one thing we can mutually agree on is that this date is over!" Matt stood up, and when he did he heard an odd *pop-pop-pop* sound as though someone were making popcorn. Then he felt a cool breeze over his torso. Looking down, he realized that his bloated belly had caused all the buttons of his shirt to pop off and was now exposed for the general public to see.

Emma laughed. She laughed so hard she snorted. She

laughed until her eyes watered. "I can't believe it!" she said between giggles. "This is the best bad date ever. Wait till I tell my girlfriends!"

Matt tried to clutch his shirt closed, and fled the premises. As soon as he hit the sidewalk, the pressure from his belly snapped his belt buckle, and he had to hold up his pants with his other hand to keep them from falling down.

He relinquished his grip on his shirt long enough to get into his car. He just needed to get home so this terrible night would be over.

Back at his apartment, Matt changed into a baggy T-shirt and a pair of elastic-waisted pajama pants. Tomorrow he would have to go shopping for new clothes. But what could he wear while he shopped? Was he going to turn into one of those tacky people who wore pajamas in public?

The pressure in his stomach was getting worse, and the weird knot on his head was hurting where it was stretching the skin of his scalp. Maybe he had some medicine that might help him. He went to the kitchen, chewed up a couple of antacid tablets, and drank a glass of water.

He waited for relief, but it didn't come. Instead, the pressure increased. Even the soft T-shirt he was wearing felt irritating. He took it off and looked down at his watermelon-shaped belly. The pressure from inside was pounding, pummeling.

He looked at the skin of his belly. There was movement underneath. When he felt the pounding, a faint imprint of an indeterminate shape showed up on his skin. Matt stifled a scream as he realized the truth: something was inside him, and it was trying to get out.

The painful pounding became more insistent, a drumbeat of agony. If it was out of him, whatever it was, the pain would stop. *Get it out, get it out*, he thought as he squeezed his eyes shut and clenched his jaw. He grabbed his discarded T-shirt and bit down on the fabric just to have some kind of outlet for the pain.

If he got it out, the pain would stop. But how? There was no place for it to go.

Another surge of pain hit him, this one crushing. He doubled over and grabbed the kitchen counter for support. His gaze turned to the kitchen knives hanging on a magnetic strip on the wall. *He could cut it out. Cutting would relieve the pressure and get whatever it was out. He would be free of whatever this burden was. He wanted to be free.*

He grabbed the largest, sharpest kitchen knife and lay on his back on the floor. Starting the incision was the hardest part, but the pain inside him was greater than any pain he could cause himself. He sank the knife's tip into the top of his abdomen and then drew the blade downward, biting down on the T-shirt so the neighbors wouldn't hear him scream.

There was pain, but there was also relief. The pressure stopped, the blood flowed, and Matt saw, emerging from the incision, one long green rabbit ear. The whole rabbit emerged, wet and slimy with mucus, a perfectly formed

Springtrap the size of a healthy, newborn infant. But unlike a newborn infant, the rabbit could pull itself out of the incision, land in a kneeling position on the kitchen floor, and then rise to stand.

The blood loss was making Matt fade in and out of consciousness, but even in his addled state, he could see that the creature he had spawned was Springtrap but somehow *not* Springtrap. This one was realer, more organic than the one in the video game. Matt's mind drifted back to a story his mom had read to him when he was little about a stuffed toy rabbit that had wished so hard to be real that it became real.

The Springtrap that stood over Matt's bleeding body was not an amalgamation of code that somebody like him had programmed into a computer. This Springtrap was *real*.

The green rabbit sat down on the floor beside Matt and rested Matt's head in its furry lap. It felt nice. Matt was losing so much blood. Could a person lose this much blood and still stay alive?

The rabbit stroked Matt's cheek. Matt didn't know if he heard the word come out of the rabbit's mouth or if it was only in his own head:

Daddy.

"So you entered the apartment and you found him like this?" The police officer was taking notes as they talked in the blood-drenched kitchen.

"Yes, officer." Jason was shaking, and he could feel his heart thudding in his chest. "I was moving out of the apartment, and I came here about ten o'clock to get my stuff."

"Ten a.m.?" the officer asked.

"Yes, sir. I thought Matt would be at work, but instead I found him . . . here." He heard the sob in his voice. He was trying to hold it together, but he wasn't succeeding.

"So you were roommates, but you were moving out of the apartment," the officer said. "Had you had a disagreement?"

"Yeah, kind of, but just a little one. Nothing that would lead me to do something like . . . this. And I mean, I'm not a violent person. I could never do something like this anyway."

Jason wished somebody would cover up the body, but even when they did, he knew he couldn't unsee it. Matt was gutted like a fish, his shirtless torso a gaping hole. Blood had gushed from the sides of the wound and now formed a large, congealing puddle on the kitchen floor. The now-bloody kitchen knife Jason had used countless times to chop vegetables was in Matt's lifeless hand.

"Did your roommate have any enemies, anyone who would wish him ill?" the officer asked.

"Well, I mean, Matt was a prickly guy, not always the easiest person to get along with. But just because he could be annoying doesn't mean that anybody wanted him dead."

The officer nodded. "Had he shown any signs of depression or suicidal thoughts?"

"I think he was kind of depressed, yeah," Jason said. "He'd had a nasty divorce and breakups from a few rebound relationships after that. I also got the feeling there was a lot of stress at work, though he wasn't the kind of person who'd talk about that kind of thing much." Jason looked down at his friend's body. It was the last thing he wanted to see, so why did he keep looking at it? "Why would someone do this to themselves?"

The officer looked up from his notes. "Well, son, in my line of work you never stop being surprised about what people are capable of." He looked down at the body, then squinted as if he was seeing something he hadn't noticed before. He put on a plastic glove, then squatted on the floor, reaching for something.

It was a clump of something green and fuzzy, like the artificial fur from a stuffed animal. "Do you have any idea what this could be?" the officer asked.

Jason looked at the unfamiliar green fur. It was covered in an unpleasant slime, like a clear mucus. "I have no idea," Jason said.

The officer rolled slimy hairs between his finger and thumb, looking at them with apparent confusion, then shrugged and wiped his hand on a clean paper towel.

THE MAN IN ROOM 1280

Standing at the smudged window in room 1280, the nurses deliberately kept their backs to their patient and watched the priest approach the hospital. They all breathed as shallowly as they could, trying to ignore the sensation of being observed . . . and judged.

"He has to be warned," one of the nurses said.

"He won't believe us," the second one said.

The head nurse's face was hard as stone. "Then he'll find out the hard way."

Arthur pedaled his vintage bicycle, Ruby, through the stone archway at the base of the drive leading up to Heracles Hospital. The archway, like much of the hospital itself, was engulfed in thick, green ivy.

The bicycle's antique balloon tires chuffed at the moist pavement, spitting fallen leaves in their wake. A black SUV passed Arthur, and the little boy in the back seat turned to stare, watching Arthur until the SUV rounded the drive's curve for the columned entrance of the imposing medical center.

Arthur knew that he and Ruby made a striking picture. Arthur didn't *have* to wear the long, flowing black cassock that fluttered out behind Ruby, but he liked wearing it. It buoyed him, made him feel like he was being lifted by angels' wings. Or maybe he just thought it looked good, in which case he needed to do better with the first deadly sin. Ruby was evidence of that as well. A priest didn't need a fully restored 1953 bicycle with gleaming chrome fenders and shiny red paint, but a priest could enjoy what he had, couldn't he? Ruby was a gift from a dying man. How could Arthur refuse to accept her?

Arthur smiled to himself. The truth was that neither his nor Ruby's appearance interested him much. He was really just a meek man who allowed himself a couple of indulgent flairs because they made him happy.

A few drops of rain hit Arthur's face, making him regret leaving his felt saturno hat, sized large enough to fit over his red bicycle helmet, at home. "It's going to rain," Arthur's housekeeper, Peggy, had warned him.

"The sun loiters behind every cloud, Peggy," he'd told her. "It just needs a little faith to coax it out."

Peggy had laughed at him . . . as she often did.

Arthur glanced up at the roiling steel-gray sky. Layered behind the gray were inky wisps of cirrus clouds that curled like beckoning fingers.

Arthur put his head down and pedaled faster. Just another couple hundred feet, and he'd be under the hospital's portico, sheltered beneath the dubious protection of the stone Cerberus statue that hunched atop the columns at the hospital's entrance.

Heracles Hospital was one of the more imposing hospitals to which Arthur had been called. The structure had been built centuries before using rough-hewn stone painstakingly extracted from the local quarry at the cost of countless men's lives, and it held generations of pain, struggle, and sorrow within its walls. But Arthur knew it also held hope and love and joy. That was always what he chose to see.

When he looked up from the road, Arthur's gaze was drawn to the sky above the hospital. He smiled. One streaming, golden ray of sunshine touched the back side of the red tile roof, spearing the blackness and slicing through the gray clouds pressing down on the building.

"See, Ruby?" Arthur said, "Like I said—it just needs a little faith."

Ruby didn't respond, but Arthur had to laugh at himself when, just as he pulled up to the bike rack under the portico, rain began to fall in heavy drops. They splatted the pavement and filled the air with a sweet ozone smell.

"Well, rain is good, too," he said as he flipped up the hem of his cassock and got off Ruby's cushy leather seat.

"Excuse me, Father? Were you talking to me?" someone said.

Arthur turned around to find a young woman in a rain slicker, her blonde hair pulled into a taut ponytail, juggling a pink backpack, an orange tote bag, and a red umbrella. She had a square face and a wide mouth that were spared from looking masculine by her lively blue eyes and the bright makeup she wore. She smiled at Arthur tentatively.

"Hello, young lady," Arthur said. He gave her a half bow.

Arthur had turned just forty-seven the previous spring, but he looked older because his hair had turned mostly gray a decade before, and deep emotions had carved lines on his face. Recently, he'd decided he was now old enough to refer to younger women as "young lady." When he was a young man himself, he was always befuddled by what to call women. "Miss" and "Ma'am" seemed to offend more often than not, for reasons that confused Arthur. "Hey you" was always inappropriate.

"Hi," the young woman said.

Arthur held out a hand. "I'm Father Blythe." Inwardly, he cringed at the formality. He preferred being called by his first name, but his bishop had made it abundantly clear that only so many of Arthur's idiosyncrasies would be tolerated.

"I'm Mia," the young woman said. She shook Arthur's hand.

Mia's hand was small, soft, and very, very cold. Arthur held it slightly longer than he should have, willing some of his warmth into the chill of her fingertips.

"Mia Fremont," Mia said when Arthur released her hand. "I'm a nurse here. Or I'm going to be. Or, I mean, I am. Well, as of fifteen minutes from now I am. I guess. Or I am because I was already hired?" Mia's voice was mellow and sweet and filled with endearing uncertainty.

Arthur smiled. "Congratulations," he said. He looked at Mia more closely and saw that a dark blue nurse's uniform was hiding under her yellow rain slicker.

"Um, thanks?" Mia looked at the hospital's entrance and frowned. Her lower lip quivered for just a second.

Arthur pulled a bicycle chain and lock from the satchel he wore slung across his body. He bent over to secure Ruby. He was all for faith, but prudence had a place in the world, too.

A car pulled in under the portico and let out a large woman barking orders at a smaller woman, who followed her into the hospital. An older couple walked slowly toward the entrance, hand in hand. A janitor sat on a nearby bench, staring at his feet. Two fat pigeons hopped along the walkway, pecking at invisible morsels.

The rain was coming down harder now. It thrummed on the pavement and hissed under the tires of passing cars. A metallic trickling sound came from the downspouts at the bottom edge of the hospital's columns.

Arthur straightened and realized Mia was still standing next to him. She stared at the hospital entrance.

"Are you okay, Mia?" Arthur asked.

Mia blinked. "What? Me? Sure. I mean, I will be. I hope. Well, yes, I'm better than I was. I . . ." She stopped and turned. "Why is the dog that guards Hades up there?" She pointed at the portico's ceiling.

Arthur frowned. He wasn't sure of that himself. In Greek mythology, Cerberus was tasked with preventing the dead from leaving the underworld. Arthur didn't know whether the Cerberus statue was meant to suggest it was going to keep the dead from entering the hospital or whether it was going to keep the people who died in the hospital from moving on. The symbolism was made even murkier by the hospital's name. Heracles, the son of Zeus and Alcmene, was a mythological hero. One of his "twelve labors" was capturing Cerberus. The hospital's name and statuary left Arthur wondering if he was in a place of good or evil. Either way, he had a job to do.

"I'm not exactly sure," Arthur said. "But it's just a statue."

Mia didn't seem convinced.

Arthur glanced at his plain black-banded watch. "Shall

we?" He indicated the hospital's automatic sliding doors, which had swished open and closed at least a dozen times since Arthur had locked up Ruby.

Mia lifted her chin. "Yes, I guess I have to." She glanced at her own watch. "I made sure to get here early, and I'm going to be late if I don't go in now."

Arthur took a step, but Mia didn't.

Arthur stopped. He wanted to get on with why he was here, but Mia seemed to need help. And helping was what Arthur did.

"Do I perceive a hesitation?" Arthur asked.

Mia sighed. "This job wasn't my first choice. I wanted the position at Glendale, you know?"

Arthur nodded. He visited Glendale Hospital often, and he had to admit that he preferred it as well. He'd only visited Heracles the one time so far, just the previous week, and he already knew this wasn't going to be his favorite place.

But Arthur couldn't be choosy. He was called to where he was called.

"Heracles is actually far more modern than Glendale," Arthur offered as encouragement.

Ten years before, Heracles had been bought by a billionaire, who practically gutted the old hospital before renovating it into a state-of-the-art medical center. The renovation made sure to keep all the original exterior architectural details, and even the hospital's interior was designed to be reminiscent of an older era, with crisp white walls, black-and-white tiled floors, thick baseboards, and crown molding. The result was a sort of time-whiplash where cutting-edge technology shared space with crystal chandeliers and wrought iron scrollwork.

"I know," Mia said. "But . . ." She sighed again. "I guess it's better than the prison hospital. That's where I was before."

Arthur was surprised. "Really? I never saw you there."

"You go out to the prison?"

"I go where I'm needed," Arthur said.

A siren screamed, squawked, then burbled into abrupt silence as an ambulance rocked to a stop in front of the hospital's emergency entrance, fifty feet from where Arthur and Mia stood.

"Shall we go inside?" Arthur suggested. He put his hand lightly on Mia's upper back in an attempt to propel her forward.

It didn't work. Mia grabbed the sleeve of Arthur's cassock. "What do you mean, you go where you're needed?"

Arthur stepped back to avoid two teenage girls carrying a bouquet of balloons that looked big enough to pick them up and carry them away. He motioned for Mia to join him next to a cluster of panicle hydrangeas, the plants' large, white cylindrical flowers hanging on valiantly even though early fall's chill pressed upon them.

Once tucked out of the way, Arthur faced Mia. "I give the dying their last rites."

Mia shivered. "But you seem so cheerful. So kind. How can you be that way and be around . . . death?"

Arthur smiled. "Death isn't a sad thing. It's a transition. And I'm kind of like a tour guide for people making the transition. Or maybe more like a traveling companion. Instead of letting fear take people away, I step in and take fear's place. Once fear is gone, the soul can reach the other side in peace."

Mia gazed into Arthur's eyes, and he wondered what she saw there. He perceived his eyes to be the boring, brown eyes of a simple man. But what did others see?

Arthur waited, sure he was still needed here more than he was needed in the hospice wing that had summoned him. At least for another moment.

Finally, Mia took a deep breath and nodded. "I'm glad I met you, Father."

"Me too, Mia."

She held up her arm, elbow out. "Well, could you escort me to my first day on the job, then? I've been assigned to the hospice wing, and I bet that's where you're going."

Arthur smiled and took Mia's arm. "Indeed I am, Mia. Let's go."

At the curved desk at the nurse's station in the hospice wing, Arthur passed Mia off to a tall, sharp-edged woman with too many teeth and a dark-eyed gaze that unsettled Arthur. Nurse Ackerman was the head of the hospice wing, and Arthur had met her last week when he came to introduce himself. He'd admonished himself for disliking her immediately, although to be fair, he doubted many human beings *did* like her. He said a silent prayer for Mia—and for Nurse Ackerman—then he followed the nurse's rigid, bony back down the wide hall.

As they passed open doorways, Arthur occasionally glanced into rooms when he felt moved to do so. Some rooms felt heavy and somber, and Arthur said a prayer for the patients and families in them. Some rooms felt ebullient, sometimes even effervescent. The people in those rooms didn't need Arthur's help—they understood the truth of the journey ahead. He prayed for them, anyway. You could never have too much support.

Nurse Ackerman led Arthur past room after room, so far down the long hall that he wondered if they'd somehow passed through an invisible barrier into another hospital. The longer they walked, the denser the air felt. The worse it smelled, too. Arthur was used to the hospital smells of bitter medicine, sharp urine, fetid waste, and pungent antiseptics. But this was something else, something acrid and ancient.

"The patient you are about to see," Nurse Ackerman said, "is a special case."

Arthur almost jumped out of his skin when Nurse Ackerman opened her mouth. He was already surprised by her escort down the hall—he hadn't expected her to speak, too. She'd barely spoken to him the last time he was here, and then only to give him a room number and send him on his way. Her voice was as sharp as her appearance, and it held a disturbing sibilance that made the hairs stand up on the back of Arthur's neck. Every consonant sounded like it was being spit on and then stabbed with a forked tongue.

She continued, "The man has been on life support for years."

"How many years?" Arthur asked.

Nurse Ackerman's shoulder blades rose in annoyance. "Irrelevant," she snapped.

"He's been here all this time?"

Nurse Ackerman ignored Arthur. "When the state finally took him off life support."

"Why did the state do that? Where's his family?"

Nurse Ackerman whirled around and impaled Arthur with a searing look. "He has no family!" she nearly shouted. Her tone suggested Arthur should have known that, somehow. Yes, he'd done a little research on this place, talked to a couple colleagues. But he hadn't heard of any special case.

Nurse Ackerman rubbed at the large mole under her left eye. She took a breath, turned away from Arthur, and resumed walking.

Arthur glanced back over his shoulder to be sure he was still in Heracles Hospital and would be able to find his way back to Ruby. At the moment, his bicycle seemed impossibly far away.

"As I was saying, the state took him off life support," Nurse Ackerman continued with the air of someone long-suffering. "Even so, he wouldn't die."

"A miracle." Arthur said a quick prayer of thanks.

"Hardly!" The word sounded like a shot, reverberating off the stark white walls and closed doors around them.

Closed doors. Arthur looked at the old-fashioned, wide, six-panel dark wood doors with frosted glass windows. All the doors were closed on this end of the hall, and none of the panels revealed light from within the rooms. Why? Arthur opened his mouth to ask, then thought better of it and remained silent.

Nurse Ackerman stopped before a door that looked strangely darker than all the other doors they had passed, but the glass panel indicated the room's light was on. He glanced up to check the overhead lights—was one of them out? Before he could confirm his suspicion, Nurse Ackerman pushed the door open. "He's in here," she said unnecessarily.

Arthur glanced at the number by the door: 1280.

As soon as the door was open, the origin of the smell Arthur had noticed was obvious. It came from whatever lay in the hospital bed on the other side of the room. Up close, the smell was even more noxious, and it was more easily discerned. It was a smoky smell but not like any smoky smell Arthur had ever encountered. It was like smelling burnt meat, smoldering plastic, and molten steel all at once. Arthur picked out the disturbing odors of carbon and sulfur. What was in this room?

Arthur didn't have long to ponder the question, because Nurse Ackerman stepped aside and made a sweeping hand gesture at the bed in front of her. She reminded Arthur of those women on game shows, the ones who elaborately indicated potential prizes.

Lying there was the man Arthur had come to see. Arthur stopped breathing. He clutched the doorjamb. He ordered his legs to keep holding him up.

This patient could not be called a prize . . . except perhaps in hell.

Arthur had seen a lot of horrible things in his tenure as a priest. He'd been to car crashes and airplane crashes and all manner of natural disasters. He'd prayed over people missing limbs, missing eyes, missing large chunks of their bodies. He'd seen so much disfigurement and physical horror that he would have, until this moment, been fairly confident in saying he'd seen every misery that could be thrust upon the human body. But this . . .

It wasn't the appearance of the man alone that took Arthur's breath away. It was . . . what?

Not the smell.

The incongruity? The impossibility?

Arthur's brain begged for oxygen, and he remembered to inhale. Sucking in a lungful of rancid, decay-tinged air, Arthur swiped at the tears that suddenly filled his eyes. They weren't emotional tears; his eyes were reacting to a puzzling acidity in the room.

Arthur worked his tongue around in his mouth, gathering up enough saliva to speak. He looked at Nurse Ackerman and noticed that her eyes were squinted and her nose was more pinched than usual.

"What's his name?" Arthur asked.

"We don't know. No family has claimed him. He has no records."

"What about fingerprints?" Arthur asked, and then immediately realized what a stupid question it was.

Nurse Ackerman let out a gurgling snort that Arthur supposed passed for a laugh.

"A DNA sample was taken, but it matches no individual in existing DNA databases," she said.

Arthur nodded.

"As you can see," Nurse Ackerman continued, "he has brain function." She gestured at a monitor upon which a series of jagged green lines played out across a dark screen. "That's a REM sleep pattern."

Arthur stared. He'd take her word for it, as the tall spiky lines meant nothing to him.

"According to Dr. Henner, the hospital's sleep expert, that particular REM pattern indicates nightmares . . . horrific nightmares."

Arthur's gaze, which had been locked on the man in the bed, whipped to Nurse Ackerman. Was there just a little too much glee in the tone she used for "horrific nightmares"?

Yes. Her mouth twitched at the corner as if she wanted to smile.

Arthur frowned, and she raised an eyebrow at him.

An overhead speaker right outside the door of room 1280 blasted out, "Nurse Ackerman, please come to room 907."

"I'll leave you to it," she said. "But I'll be back. There's more for us to discuss."

They were discussing? Arthur didn't feel like he was discussing anything. All he was doing was trying to accept what his senses were telling him. He was also trying to remember his training, his humanity, and his decency.

Nurse Ackerman's footsteps slapped the floor as she retreated down the hall. Arthur didn't let go of the doorjamb.

He knew he needed to. He had to enter the room.

But not yet.

First, he wanted to see if he could get his brain to understand the facts his eyes reported as being real. A disconnect had to be bridged before he could step into the situation and do something, anything, besides whimper like a small child.

The man—Really? Could Arthur truly call this a man? Wasn't it more corpse than man? Well, no. Some of the facts weren't consistent with a designation of corpse—the REM monitor, for example.

Fact one, the man appeared to be burned to a crisp. What lay in the bed in room 1280 resembled a human being only vaguely, in that it had the requisite shape. It had a head, a torso, two arms, and two legs. There, the similarity to humans ended.

Fact two. The burning had been so pervasive, so complete, that the only thing remaining was essentially a charred skeleton. Almost. Actually, Arthur wished the man was just a charred skeleton. If he were simply blackened human bones, he'd have been easier to look at. But the ruinous fire damage could be seen throughout the body. Although he had no hair, the man did have skin, or . . . was it skin? Arthur had never seen anything like the dermis on this man. It looked like fire had scorched away so many layers that his skin was just an ashy covering far too translucent for comfort. Arthur guessed that fire had siphoned all moisture from the body's covering, leaving it with extensive cracks, like the surface of a dried-up lakebed. Through those cracks, Arthur caught unwelcome glimpses of uncharred tissue.

Fact three. The man's organs worked, at least the ones Arthur could see. And that in itself was repellent in ways Arthur had never experienced before. Through the translucent skin's cracks, Arthur could literally watch this man's desiccated and blackened heart pumping. He could see the heat-shriveled lungs expanding and contracting. He could glimpse the seared kidneys and a bladder so carbonized it seemed like it was about to collapse in on itself.

Fact four. The man had no face. A hole in his skull indicated where his nose used to be. Dark cavernous pits lacking eyes looked at nothing. A toothless mouth gaped without lips to protect it.

Fact five. The man did have a brain. The REM pattern suggested this, and unfortunately Arthur could see bits of gray matter between the cracks in the man's burned cranium.

Fact six. The man had blood flowing in his veins. What looked like scorched worms creeped above and through toasted tissues, pulsing under the skin and around the crisp skeleton. Arthur assumed these were veins. The blood on the sheets seemed to confirm it.

Fact seven—and this was the most disturbing fact of all. It was the culmination of the other facts. It was the fact that Arthur couldn't fit into his understanding of the world, his understanding of the universe, his understanding of the power that governed everything. This was the fact that this man was alive against all odds.

What *was* he?

Arthur returned to his original question. Was this patient a man? Again, brain function would suggest he was. But what truly determined humanity and life?

The soul.

Did this gruesome collection of bloody, incinerated human remains have a soul?

Arthur decided it was time to enter the room. After all, it was his job to find out.

Peeling his fingers from the doorjamb and rubbing them to put life back into them, he took a hesitant step forward. Arthur could hear the suck and rush of his respiration even over the sound of the monitor's rhythmic beeps and the wheeze and click of the man's implausible breathing.

Stopping, Arthur looked around the room for the first time since Nurse Ackerman had opened the door. There wasn't much to see.

The room was white walled, like every other room in Heracles Hospital. The man's bed sat in the middle of the room, surrounded by monitors. On one side of the bed, an IV pole held one pouch of . . . what? Fluids? Nutrients? Did this man need either? An IV line ran into a port taped to the man's radius, or his ulna—Arthur couldn't tell from where he stood. Even though he wasn't on life support, the man did have electrical leads affixed to his head and his heart. It was surreal to see this life-affirming equipment attached to what looked like something in a morgue. The man even had a pulse-ox monitor on his left index finger bone. How was that working?

Pushed off to one side of the bed, a high-backed, padded vinyl visitor's chair was next to an empty rolling tray. The chair was positioned so its user could see out the narrow window that overlooked Heracles Hospital's parking lot. The wall opposite the window held a whiteboard; in other rooms, you might see medication schedules written there, but this one was clean. Next to the whiteboard, an LED X-ray viewer hung on the wall.

When Arthur stepped over to the window, he looked out and saw the long driveway he and Ruby had pedaled up just twenty minutes before.

Why did it feel like that had happened in another reality? Maybe in another lifetime?

Standing by the window, Arthur suddenly felt an icy rawness bore a hole through the middle of his back. The feeling was so powerful that Arthur spun around, awkwardly reaching behind himself and trying to rub the assaulted area. What was that? It had felt like something was trying to reach into his soul.

"You felt it, didn't you?" Nurse Ackerman was back.

"Felt what?" Arthur asked.

"You know what."

Arthur ignored the nurse and sat down in the vinyl chair. He couldn't look at the man again quite yet, so he looked at Nurse Ackerman. Her uniform pants were too short. He could see her black socks and an inch or so of white skin between them and the hem of her pants.

"We'd be remiss if we didn't warn you," she said.

"We?"

"Myself, Nurse Thomas, and Nurse Colton. We've worked in the hospice wing the longest. We know what he"—she wrinkled her nose at the word—"what *that* is."

"And what is it . . . h-he?" Arthur stammered.

"Evil, Father Blythe. Evil pure and simple."

Arthur shook his head. "Just because he looks like that—"

"That's not the evil," Nurse Ackerman cut in. She waved her hand at the revolting mass in the bed.

"Then what is?"

"It's what's inside of that."

"Inside? As in, under the bones? In the organs?"

Nurse Ackerman flicked her hand as if Arthur was asking stupid questions. "Who cares? It's *in* there." She shook her head and sighed. "I knew you wouldn't believe me."

Opening a file Arthur hadn't even noticed she was holding, she crossed to the X-ray viewer. There, she slapped three brain scan images into place and pointed. "Look."

Arthur gingerly stepped around the man's bed as if it might attack him.

Nurse Ackerman lifted her chin toward the brain scans. "See? There," she pointed at one part of the scan, "and there."

Arthur leaned forward. He had no idea what he was looking at. "I'm sorry. You need to explain."

Nurse Ackerman sighed. "These are coronal, sagittal, and cross-sectional scans of the man's brain. You can see the same thing in all of them."

Arthur couldn't. So he said, "You'll need to tell me what we're seeing."

She sighed again. "Our brains have four lobes, the frontal, parietal, occipital, and temporal." She tapped areas on each of the scans. "Unless a brain has a tumor or damage from a trauma like an injury or a stroke, signals in each of the four lobes should be relatively coherent. Although this man shows no sign of tumors or brain injury, the lobes' signals aren't coherent." She tapped the scans again.

Arthur focused on the sagittal scan, which showed the man's brain in profile. There he could see what looked like two different colors or textures in each area. He pointed at them. "Is that what you're talking about?"

Nurse Ackerman nodded. "The doctors believe *each lobe* of this man's brain has two distinct electromagnetic signals. This is unheard of."

"What does it mean?" Arthur asked.

Nurse Ackerman made a clucking sound. "The doctors claim they don't know. But we know."

"We?"

She gave him an eye roll that clearly indicated he was daft. "Me and my fellow nurses."

"What do you think it is?"

"We don't *think*. We *know*."

"What do you know?"

"Two signals," she jabbed each lobe, "means two living things. Two entities. They're both vying for control of the brain; that's why they're present in all of the lobes. But they're at odds with each other. We think they're tormenting each other."

Arthur had no idea what to say to that, so he blurted out the first thing that came to his mind. "Where's the evil?"

Nurse Ackerman threw up her hands. Then she waved at the scans. "There! How can one brain have competing signals? It's the very playground of evil."

Arthur thought maybe Nurse Ackerman should visit a different wing of the hospital, perhaps the psychiatric wing. But no, that wasn't kind. He should have more empathy for the woman. Anyone who was taking care of the man in this room was entitled to have a crazy theory or two. At least she and the other nurses *had* a theory. Arthur had nothing.

Nothing but his faith.

"Every man has good in him," Arthur said.

"That's not a man!"

"Okay. Every living creature has good in it."

Nurse Ackerman reached out and yanked the scans from the viewing box. "I knew you wouldn't listen."

Arthur turned and looked at the . . . man . . . in the bed. "It's my job to see the good."

Nurse Ackerman only shook her head and walked out of the room.

Mia pulled a flimsy, beige plastic chair out from one of the round tables in the staff break room. The room contained a small fridge, a counter, a microwave, and half a dozen tables with chairs; it smelled like barbecue sauce and spoiled cheese. If Mia hadn't been so hungry, the smells would have ruined her appetite. But she'd worked up an appetite so strong she could have eaten her lunch in a sewage treatment plant.

Mia opened her bag lunch and pulled out the turkey sandwich her boyfriend had made her that morning. He was so sweet! She set up her paperback thriller in front of her and popped open a cola. She took a bite of the sandwich and washed it down with cola, noticing the Dos and Don'ts posters tacked all over the plain white walls. They didn't make her feel welcome, nor did they make her feel any better about her decision to take this job.

It was a stepping stone, right? That's what her boyfriend said. "Keep your nose clean. Do a good job, and you'll be moving on up in no time," he said.

Mia took another bite of sandwich and chewed appreciatively.

That's when her new boss, Nurse Ackerman, and the other two bigwig nurses on the hospice wing marched in. Mia immediately dropped her head and pretended to be reading.

"How long has he been in there?" Nurse Thomas asked, plopping into a chair at the table behind Mia. Mia could smell her lavender-heavy perfume.

"Father Blythe?" Nurse Ackerman said. "All morning. Moron."

Two chairs scraped the floor and Mia knew the other two nurses had sat, too. Nurse Colton was right behind Mia. Already, Mia had noticed several times that Nurse Colton needed a stronger deodorant.

Mia had already planned on listening to whatever the nurses said, but when she heard Father Blythe's name combined with "moron," she tuned in more closely. Father Blythe was the very nice priest who had walked her up here to start her new job. He'd been so kind and patient with her. He was cute, too, not in a boyfriend kind of way but in an adorable old man kind of way. Short and slight with thick wavy gray hair and gentle brown eyes, Father Blythe looked like the grandfather Mia wished she had. She'd liked him immediately, and it made her mad to hear someone call him names.

Nurse Ackerman was the moron.

Mia had learned early on in nursing school that not all

nurses were nice. Some were so unpleasant Mia wondered why they'd gone into nursing in the first place. But Nurse Ackerman was the worst she'd met so far. The woman was just plain icky. Never smiling, stalking around firing orders, Nurse Ackerman showed immediately that Mia wasn't going to get anything from her new boss except for criticism and judgment. And what was it with using last names?

"We use surnames on this wing, Nurse Fremont," Nurse Ackerman said when Mia had introduced herself with a friendly "I'm Mia."

Fine. Mia didn't want to be friends, anyway.

And then there was Nurse Thomas. She was nice enough, but there wasn't much *there* there. Mia wondered how Nurse Thomas managed to keep her job. Round and sweet looking with curly graying black hair, Nurse Thomas looked like she should be at home baking cookies. She called everyone "Sweetie," and she loved to pat people on the back, but she wouldn't remember to bring her feet along if they weren't attached at the ankles. Already that morning, Mia had spent what seemed like half her shift finding things that Nurse Thomas had lost.

Nurse Colton was the only reasonably normal nurse Mia had met so far. In her midforties, Mia guessed, Nurse Colton was an athletic-looking woman with brown hair chopped short in a boyish cut, and a great tan. She was nice enough, Mia supposed, but she was too serious, as if she had something heavy on her mind.

Mia picked up her sandwich to take another bite.

"What did you tell him?" Nurse Colton asked Nurse Ackerman.

"What we know. I told him there's evil inside the man."

Mia held the sandwich in front of her face. *Evil?*

"He refuses to see it, of course," Nurse Ackerman said dismissively.

"Well, we know better, don't we, sweeties," Nurse Thomas said. "I can barely think about it without being so scared I want to throw up."

"Yes, we know better," Nurse Colton said.

Nurse Ackerman got up and plucked a plastic bag of carrots from the fridge. *No wonder she's so skinny*, Mia thought.

"He's idealistic," Nurse Ackerman said.

"I am, too," Nurse Thomas said, "but when the writing's on the wall, it's on the wall."

Mia took a bite of her sandwich and willed herself to be invisible.

"He's new," Nurse Colton said. "He'll catch on."

"I'm not so sure. He's determined," Nurse Ackerman said.

"Time will tell," Nurse Thomas said. "It always does."

The nurses chatted for a few more minutes about some of the patients Mia had already met. She wondered about the man with evil inside. Was he a patient? He must be if Father Blythe was here visiting him. Or maybe Father Blythe was visiting someone else. Mia listened, but she never heard another word about the priest. Did she need to find him and warn him? But warn him about what? It sounded like he'd already been warned and didn't believe the warning.

Arthur had been sitting in the vinyl visiting chair for over three hours. During that time, he'd accomplished little, except that he could now look at the man in the bed without nearly losing his breakfast. This made him feel slightly better about himself, but the self-congratulation was unearned. Arthur knew his belly was empty now, so he had no breakfast to lose.

And he had no business being pleased, either. He hadn't yet been able to approach the man's bed. He was still completely repulsed not just by the man but by the bloody sheets he lay on and whatever it was that was leaking from the tubes that snaked out from underneath him, attached to heavens-knew-where. Those tubes curled off the bed and ran into bags hanging from the bed's frame. Arthur could hear the body waste dribbling into plastic bags that were, regrettably, see-through. Arthur didn't venture a look.

Ever since Nurse Ackerman had left, Arthur hadn't said one word out loud. All he'd done was stare and pray.

Now he decided he had to do something else. What if the man wanted to communicate?

Arthur had no idea how or even whether it was possible, but he had to give the man a chance. Sitting in this chair, five feet from the bed, was not giving the man a chance.

Arthur took a deep breath and scooted the chair a foot closer.

"Yes, that's very brave," Arthur muttered to himself. He chuckled.

One of the monitors let out an unusual beep, or rather a normal beep at an unexpected time. In three hours, Arthur had learned the monitor's rhythm, and just now that rhythm had varied. Was it because he talked?

Breathing shallowly through his mouth—because the closer he got to the man, the worse the smells were—Arthur dragged the chair nearer to the bed. It made a screeching sound on the floor, but the monitors didn't react to that.

Arthur got the chair to within a foot of the bed, just outside the distance he thought the man could reach. He knew it wasn't friendly or caring, but Arthur wasn't ready to risk touching or being touched by the man yet.

In the three hours he'd sat here, he'd realized that a part of him, a truly traitorous part of him, half believed what Nurse Ackerman had said. Was something evil keeping the man alive?

Just thinking that disturbed him greatly. How could he be a priest and believe that evil had more power over the body than good? What if something good was keeping the man alive? Wasn't that more believable? Of course it was, he told himself.

It was divine energy that created worlds. Couldn't that energy sustain life beyond the time when life was viable? Certainly it could. Although, Arthur's logical side argued, divine energy wasn't the only kind of energy in the world.

"Stop it," Arthur admonished himself.

And the monitors beeped out of rhythm again.

"You can hear me?" Arthur asked, scooching the chair closer to the bed in spite of himself.

The monitor's beeps stuttered. The man in the bed didn't move.

Arthur leaned forward. "My name's Father Blythe. No. Forget that. My name is Arthur. Is there anything I can do for you? I want to help."

The monitors beeped erratically for several seconds.

Arthur said a silent prayer, asking for strength. *Divest me of habitual notions of what is and isn't good, what is and isn't possible. Let me see past what my senses are telling me. Give me the strength to see this man as the love I know he is, and help me interact with him accordingly.*

Arthur sat still and took several slow breaths before reaching out and taking the man's scorched finger bones in his hand. It required every ounce of his heart not to recoil at the dry, crispy phalanges in his hand. He felt like he was holding hands with a tree branch that had just come through a forest fire. No, that wasn't true. It was worse than that by far. Because, in addition to the knobby hard objects in his hand, he could feel the pulsing slither of the man's veins beneath the parched skin covering.

Give me strength, Arthur prayed again.

He must have gotten it. That was the only explanation for why he didn't scream when the finger bones and veins he held *moved*.

He did, however, drop the hand. He was human, after all.

Was it because he was polite, or because he was afraid of whatever entity had moved the fingers?

Entity? What was he thinking? This wasn't an entity. This was a man in hideous circumstances. This wasn't a foe to be vanquished. It—*he*—was a human being, worthy of love.

"You are loved," Arthur said. He could feel the truth of his words. Couldn't he?

Actually, he wasn't sure. He usually felt a flush of warmth and a surge of lightness when he said those words. But now? Nothing.

The man, however, felt something. He must have. Because he began moving his index finger.

At first, Arthur thought the finger motions were random, reflexes caused by nerves firing indiscriminately. But then he realized the finger motion was purposeful.

"Could you do that again?" he asked.

He didn't let himself wonder how the man could hear him. The man had no ears, and Arthur didn't want to look into the tortured tissue at the side of the man's skull to see if his eardrums and whatever else made it possible to translate vibration into sound were still intact.

Apparently the man could hear him, because the finger repeated the motion. Arthur watched closely.

"It's an F!" he said excitedly when he realized the finger had just written that letter in the air.

The finger stopped. Arthur took that to be affirmation.

"Just a second." Arthur dug in his satchel and pulled out

a small pad of paper and a pencil. Opening the pad, he wrote down, *F*.

"Okay. I'm ready."

Would the finger move again?

Yes!

This time it traced an *A* in the air.

"What in the name of all that's good and holy are you doing?" Nurse Ackerman yelled from the doorway.

Arthur fumbled the pencil, and it fell from his fingers. When he bent over to pick it up, he bumped his head on the bed frame. He also inhaled the odor of whatever fluid was draining from the man on the bed. It smelled like a cross between bile and vomit, and Arthur's gag reflex activated. He stood and backed away from the bed, facing the nurse, trying not to vomit.

"He's communicating!" Arthur announced.

Nurse Ackerman strode into the room. "I can see that!" she said. "And what makes you think that's a good idea?"

"Well, it's a breakthrough! It's progress. Progress is always good."

"If you think that, you're dumber than you look."

Arthur chose to ignore her.

"Do you even know what he's communicating?" Nurse Ackerman asked. "For all you know, he could be hexing you."

Hexing him? Arthur kept his face blank.

But Nurse Ackerman had a point. What was the man trying to communicate? Would it ever be clear?

"Well, let's find out," Arthur said.

"We should have called a different priest," Nurse Ackerman snapped.

"Just ignore her," Arthur said to the man in the bed. He sat back down and repositioned his pencil over the pad. "Give me the next letter."

The finger moved again. Nurse Ackerman gasped and began murmuring under her breath.

Arthur wrote down, Z.

FAZ?

"Okay," he said. "Let's keep going."

Arthur had written down "FAZBENTERDI" by the time Nurse Ackerman returned to the room. This time, she wasn't alone. She had two other nurses with her.

Both in the same dark blue uniform, the other nurses also wore similar openmouthed, wide-eyed expressions. They were obviously appalled by what the man was doing. One of the nurses, a round, grandmotherly-looking woman, covered her mouth with a hand. The other nurse, a tanned woman who looked like she spent the weekends mountain climbing, put her hands on her hips and glared at Arthur. He hoped she wasn't going to get aggressive with him, because she could take him without breaking a sweat.

They didn't say anything, though, so Arthur kept going.

One letter at a time, the man spelled out his communication in the air. When he was done, completion indicated by no further finger bone movement, Arthur had a

string of incomprehensible letters on his pad:
FAZBENTERDISCENTER.

FAZBENTERDISCENTER? What did that mean?

Arthur frowned at the letters, inserting slashes between various sets. He tried several combinations:

FAZBEN TERDIS CENTER

FAZ BENTER DIS CENTER

FAZB ENTER DISCENTER

FA ZB ENTER DIS CENTER

"I think I have the CENTER right," he mumbled to himself. "But the other parts?" He tapped his pencil on his pad.

Wait. What if he'd missed letters? It had been hard to interpret the motions of the bony finger. "Okay, so what if . . ." Arthur played with the letters some more, landing finally on: FAZB ENTER DIS CENTER.

Arthur thought back over "DIS CENTER"—he'd seen that abbreviation before with some of the charities he'd worked with. "Distribution Center!" Arthur shouted. It had to be.

But what was FAZB ENTER?

"I need a phone book," he told the nurses, who remained at the foot of the bed watching Arthur as if he was a live reality show. "I need to look up FAZB ENTER."

"Fazbear Entertainment," the grandmotherly nurse whispered.

"What?" Arthur asked.

"Quiet, Nurse Thomas," Nurse Ackerman hissed.

Nurse Thomas covered her mouth with a plump hand. But it was too late. Arthur processed what she'd said.

"Fazbear Entertainment Distribution Center!" Arthur cried out in glee. "This is amazing!"

He turned to look at the nurses. They were all pale, even the tanned one, and they all stared at him and the man in the bed with obvious dread.

"This is remarkable!" Arthur said. "Has he ever done anything like this before?"

"Certainly not!" Nurse Ackerman shook her head. "You don't understand the forces you're playing with."

"Forces?"

Arthur decided he'd had enough of the nurses. He turned back to the man.

"Let's see. How you can tell me what this place means to you?" Arthur thought for a second. He considered asking the man to air-write why he had just given Arthur the name of this place, but that could take hours, and Arthur figured the man didn't have the strength for that. Given that he should have been dead long ago, lengthy communications didn't seem like a good idea.

Plus, as excited as he was, Arthur really needed to leave this room. It seemed to him that the sulfur smell was getting stronger, and now there was a hint of a feces odor wafting up from the bed. Did the man's bowels work? Arthur hadn't wondered before, and he wasn't going to look now.

"I have an idea," he said, relieved that he did indeed have an idea.

He could hear the nurses whispering in the doorway. He blocked them out.

"Why don't I make guesses about why this place is important to you? When I get to the right one, you can either raise a finger or just react so the monitors pick it up."

The monitors hiccuped, and Arthur took that to be assent. He threw out his first guess.

"It's where you used to work."

Nothing.

"You have family there."

Nope.

"You have unfinished business there."

No reaction.

"You hid something there."

That guess made Arthur smile. It was a dead giveaway that he loved mystery and adventure books and movies.

Arthur noticed the nurses had come farther into the room. Now they stood in a semicircle a couple feet from the end of the bed. Arthur wondered why they were still here. If they thought what he was doing was so abhorrent, why didn't they just leave?

"It was the last place you were before you got hurt."

No movement. No monitor reaction.

"You need something from there."

Nothing.

"You've always wanted to go there."

The monitors blipped so infinitesimally Arthur thought he was imagining it. But what if he wasn't?

"Is this a place you want to go?"

The monitors reacted.

"He can't go anyplace, sweetie," the round nurse said. "He can only go, well, someplace other than earth."

Arthur stood and walked over to the nurses. "You mean hell?" he whispered.

Nurse Ackerman gave him one sharp head nod.

The tanned nurse said, "Well, duh."

And the monitors in the room went crazy. Beeps were sounding so fast, they blurred together into one long screech.

Arthur turned back to the man. He suddenly understood. "You want to go to this place before you die."

The monitors all fell silent. Completely silent.

For five seconds, the only sound in the room was the combined breathing of Arthur, the nurses, and the man.

And then the monitors started beeping in a normal rhythm again.

Arthur turned back to the nurses. "He wants to go to Fazbear Entertainment Distribution Center before he dies."

"Impossible," Nurse Ackerman said.

Arthur sat in a low-slung dark-blue visitor's chair in front of a cluttered desk that belonged to the assistant of the assistant of the Heracles Hospital administrator. Judging from the man's (boy's?) age, Arthur suspected he was more than two people removed from the person in charge. But that was okay. Arthur knew how to climb bureaucratic ladders.

"So I'm not sure what you want?" the assistant's assistant said. His name was Peter Fredericks. "Call me Pete," he'd told Arthur.

Pete's desk was in a corner cubicle in a room of similar cubicles nowhere near the Heracles Hospital administrator's office. Most of the people in the cubicles were talking on the phone. Those who weren't on the phone were typing on their keyboards; the room was filled with half conversations and the click-click of typing.

Arthur filtered out the sounds and focused on Pete. "As I said, Pete, I want to know if there's anything in the file of the man in room 1280 that indicates why he might want to go to Fazbear Entertainment Distribution Center before he dies."

"Well, yes, you said that." Pete scratched the sparse facial hair on his chin. It appeared to be a failing attempt at a goatee, probably intended to cover up the acne there. "But I don't know why you want to know," Pete said in a voice that hadn't yet found an adult depth of tone.

"I want to know because it might help me make it happen for him."

"The man in room 1280 can't be moved." When Pete said "man in room 1280," he looked down at his desk and chewed on his cuticles with great concentration.

"So I've been told. But nothing is impossible," Arthur replied.

"Moving, uh, him, is."

Arthur braced his hands on the too-soft cushion under his butt and maneuvered himself, with effort, forward in his seat. "Pete, isn't the very existence of the man in room 1280 proof that nothing is impossible? If he can be in that room, still breathing, still able to communicate a desire, might it not be possible to fulfill that desire for him? Think about it, Pete."

Pete glanced up at Arthur. His face was as white as the walls in the tiny cubicle. Pete was clearly thinking about the man in 1280 . . . and he didn't want to be. He looked down again, and he tapped the very thin file folder on the desk in front of him. An open container of Chinese food tipped against a stack of thicker folders and threatened to spill its contents. From the aroma, Arthur guessed it was sweet and sour chicken.

"Well, there's nothing in here, nothing about, uh, Fazbear anything."

"I see," Arthur said. He battled the chair for a few seconds and finally managed to stand. "Well then, I'll need to talk to someone who can give me permission to take the man to the Fazbear Entertainment Distribution Center. I assume that's not you."

Pete stood, bumped the thick stack of files on his desk and spilled the Chinese food. Yep. Sweet and sour chicken.

Pete ignored the sticky mess on his desk and scurried

after Arthur as he turned to leave. Grabbing the sleeve of Arthur's cassock, Pete said, "No one's going to give you permission."

"We'll see," Arthur said.

Arthur stepped out of the hospital and stood under the portico. He watched mist waft sideways in a steady southerly breeze. He and Ruby would be soaked by the time they got home. Not in a hurry to start his wet, cold journey, he scanned the black-and-silver mottled sky. There were no rays of sun to be seen now. Twilight hovered.

Arthur took a deep breath of rain-cleansed air. He'd need a year's worth of such breaths to clear his olfactory system from the torments it had endured today. It wasn't kind to think about how bad the man in room 1280 smelled, but Arthur couldn't help it. After over seven hours by the man's side, he thought the smell might never leave him again.

Nurse Ackerman had tried to get Arthur to leave right after the man's communication breakthrough, but Arthur had refused. He spent the next three hours sitting with the man, praying, asking for help. Arthur needed to know if he was simply helping a tortured soul or . . . something else.

He never got a clear answer, so in the absence of definitive evidence to the contrary, he chose to stay positive: this was a man who needed his help.

"Hi, Father, I mean, Father Blythe."

Arthur smiled. "Mia!" he said as he turned. "How was your first day of work?"

Arthur could probably have answered the question for her. Her ponytail had slid lower on her head, and dozens of strands had come loose to fly around her face. She kept blowing one of them away from her nose. Her mascara was smudged, and there was a blackish stain on her uniform.

"It was okay, I guess. Well, not okay exactly. My dad used to say when I asked him that question, 'Well, Miamymia' . . . that's what he called me, all one word like it was my name, he'd say, 'Well, Miamymia, it was a day.' So I guess I had a day. It was a day."

Arthur nodded. "Sometimes all we can do is have a day."

Mia tilted her head and studied Arthur. "I think you had a day, too? Maybe?"

Arthur nodded. "That I did."

A group of boisterous men in soccer uniforms converged on the portico. They were mud and grass stained, and appeared to be celebrating a victory as they charged toward the hospital entrance. Arthur guessed one of their teammates had gotten injured.

Mia stepped closer to Arthur when one of the men whistled at her. Arthur ushered her back to the friendly panicle hydrangeas they'd stood next to that morning.

Morning.

Arthur couldn't believe he'd spent the whole day at Heracles. Peggy would be furious with him. He'd called her to have her reschedule his other appointments for the day. Now he was going to have to tell her to reschedule the rescheduling.

"Have you been here all day?" Mia asked.

"I was just thinking about that. Yes, I have. It wasn't my plan, but—"

"Man plans. God laughs." Mia giggled, then covered her mouth. "Oh, I hope that's not like an insult or something for a priest?"

Arthur laughed. "No. Not at all."

They stood in silence and watched cars coming and going under the portico. They both coughed when a loud diesel engine belched exhaust three feet away.

Arthur's stomach growled, and he realized he hadn't eaten anything but a protein bar since he'd left the rectory. But Mia looked like she wanted to say something, so he lingered. Plus, he was just enjoying being in relatively fresh air looking at a lovely human being.

"Father Blythe?"

"Yes, Mia?"

"Can I ask you something?"

"Of course."

Mia looked around, then stepped closer to Arthur. Her hair smelled like ammonia, but her breath smelled like peppermint.

"Father, do you believe in evil?"

Arthur raised an eyebrow. "I do."

"Do you think there's evil . . . in there?" Mia lifted a shoulder in the direction of the hospital.

Arthur frowned. He believed evil was everywhere. But so was good. The eternal battle was waged daily, all over the world.

"Why do you ask?"

Mia wrinkled her nose and twisted her mouth. "Can I ask another question?"

Arthur nodded.

"Did you spend the day with someone in the hospice wing?"

Arthur's frown grew deeper. What was she digging for?

Well, telling her he was on the wing didn't reveal any confidences. "Yes, I did. Why?"

Mia opened her eyes wide. Arthur could almost hear her brain cells shifting gears. "I don't know about the nurses on that wing. I mean, besides me, but I don't feel like I'm really one of them yet. It's the others, you know. Nurse Ackerman and Nurse Colton and Nurse Thomas."

"Ah."

"So it's just that—"

At that moment a zippy red sports car whipped into the driveway under the portico and beeped its horn. Mia's face lit up when she saw it. "That's my boyfriend!" She blew the good-looking young man behind the wheel a kiss. She turned back to Arthur. "Um, sorry. I need to go."

"Of course."

Mia took a step toward the red car.

"But Mia?"

She turned.

"Some people have closed minds. Always keep yours open."

She looked at him, her face as solemn as he'd seen it. "I will," she promised. "Bye, Father Blythe."

"Bye, Mia."

Arthur watched the sports car whiz away, and he thought about the man in room 1280. His attempt to get answers in the hospital administration office, and his brush-off by Pete, made it clear Arthur wasn't going to find out why the man wanted to go to the Fazbear Entertainment Distribution Center. But no matter. That wasn't Arthur's business. It was just his job to ensure the man got there.

However, that was easier said than done. Pete and Nurse Ackerman weren't the only ones at Heracles Hospital who thought such a trip was impossible. Arthur had a battle ahead. He just hoped he was on the right side of it.

Mia's second day of work started weirdly.

Unable to find her fellow nurses when she arrived at the nursing station for her assignments, Mia just shrugged and went from room to room checking on her patients.

Mia didn't love taking care of hospice patients, because she had too much empathy for the families. She knew they often suffered even more than the patients. But she did find the work satisfying when she did it right. She wouldn't have minded the new job so much if it wasn't for the other nurses . . . and the other thing . . .

Mia shook her head and strode briskly down the hall.

Popping in and out of rooms, she checked IVs, adjusted pillows, filled pitchers, and emptied urine collection bags. When she reached the last room she'd been told to attend to the day before, room 1200, she wondered why the rest of the doors on the strangely long hall were closed.

She lingered in the hallway just outside the last open door. A storage room was across from her, its door slightly open. Then Mia saw a shadow flit past that opening.

Sucking in a deep breath, Mia tiptoed across the hall, making sure her crepe soles didn't squeak on the tiles. She hesitated outside the storage room. She was about to open the door and investigate when she heard voices.

She knew immediately that she'd found her fellow nurses. Mia was about to walk in and ask what was going on, but then she heard the word "kill."

Mia went as still and silent as the floor she stood on. She took a stealthy step to the wall and pressed against it as she put her ear to the sliver of an opening at the hinge side of the door.

"I suppose we must," Nurse Thomas said.

"Someone has to do it," Nurse Colton said. "I don't have a problem with it. It's not like murder, because it's not human."

"It's extermination," said Nurse Ackerman. "We're doing nothing more or less than ridding the hospital of vermin."

"Oh, I think it's much more," Nurse Thomas said, "don't you? Killing rats or cockroaches is good, of course. But ridding the world of evil? That's more than pest removal.

That's a calling. It's, well, it's heroic!" Nurse Thomas's voice had climbed to a new level of self-righteousness.

Heroic? Mia's fingers twitched. She wanted so bad to throw the door open and ask what these three odd women were talking about.

"Well, I agree with you both," Nurse Ackerman said, "but others won't see it quite the same way. Technically, he's one of our patients."

They were going to kill a patient?

Mia looked around. What should she do?

"They don't pay me enough to call that . . . thing . . . a patient," Nurse Colton said. "I don't need people to understand. I know what's right. Killing evil is right."

Nurse Colton must have been standing close to the door, because her body odor nearly blotted out the smells of bleach and wood polish that usually emanated from the storage room. Mia hoped she didn't have any telltale odors or scents herself. She caught the end of her ponytail and inhaled, but she only got a faint whiff of her conditioner.

"Absolutely," Nurse Thomas continued.

Mia dropped her ponytail and returned to listening.

"Then we're agreed," Nurse Ackerman said.

The women must have been nodding, because they went silent.

"I'll be the one who does it. I'm head nurse. It's my responsibility," Nurse Ackerman declared.

"We'll do whatever you need us to do," Nurse Colton offered.

"I'll need morphine," Nurse Ackerman said.

"I can fudge the tracking," said Nurse Colton.

"We can take a little here and a little there from the other patients," Nurse Thomas added.

"We have to hurry," Nurse Ackerman said. "We don't know how quickly that priest will move. He's determined enough to get the hospital to cave, and we have to get this done before the . . . thing . . . in room 1280 can leave."

The nurses must have nodded again, and now Mia could hear faint rustles from inside the storage room. She decided she'd better go.

Pushing off from the wall, Mia took a step. And that's when she saw what she'd been trying to convince herself she hadn't seen before.

A little boy slithered out from the storage room. He came sideways through the slim door opening.

Mia slapped a hand over her mouth to stifle a scream. She gritted her teeth, exasperated with herself. She'd had the same reaction when she'd seen this boy just the day before. But he was only a little boy, a cute and playful little boy! With his curly black hair and rosy cheeks, the boy's adorable factor was diminished, slightly, by just two things. First, he wore a cheap alligator mask that covered his forehead and his eyes; the gator's mouth rested on the boy's impish nose. Second, the boy had a toothy grin, just a little too devilish to be endearing, one notch past acceptable on the scale of mischief. But he was a little boy, and little boys liked to look like this. Mia's cousin, Lucas, was a case in point. That child always looked like he was up to no good, and he usually was.

So why did this boy make Mia want to scream?

Before she could answer her own question, the boy winked at her and scampered down the hall. Mia turned to watch, but realized the nurses were about to exit.

Mia darted toward the open door of the last patient she'd attended before loitering outside the storage room, looking for the boy again. But he was gone.

When Mia burst into room 1200, Mr. Nolan, the room's occupant, looked up from his crossword puzzle. "Hello, Nurse Fremont," he said, "how fortuitous. What is another word for hell? Six letters, starts with an S."

"Shades," Mia blurted, wondering why the word was on the tip of her tongue.

Mr. Nolan, whose gaunt face was haunted by the sunken eyes of the soon-to-be-gone-from-this-world, slowly wrote in his puzzle book. "Exactly right. You're an angel."

It took two days for Nurse Ackerman to acquire enough morphine for her task. At least she hoped it was enough— she wasn't actually sure what enough was, in this case. Normal treatment dosages versus overdoses had never been relevant to the man in room 1280. Nothing about him was normal, so there was no reason to assume medication would affect him the same as it would other *humans* of his size and weight. Allowing for this, Nurse Ackerman and her colleagues gathered enough extra morphine to kill an entire wing of evil patients. She figured she'd start with what she thought might work and add to it as necessary.

As soon as she had a quantity of morphine that gave her at least some level of confidence in the success of her mission, she didn't waste any time. A friend who worked in admin had informed Nurse Colton that Father Blythe was being relentless in his campaign to get the man in room 1280 to Fazbear Entertainment Distribution Center.

Nurse Ackerman strode down the long hallway, her rubber soles smacking the tiles. Her thoughts about Father Blythe made her footsteps even louder than usual. She clenched her fists. She was so *angry* with the man.

How could Father Blythe be so clueless and blind? Couldn't he see he was being duped, being used as a tool for wickedness? Wasn't the very place the man wanted to visit a clue?

Nurse Ackerman had researched Fazbear Entertainment, and she was alarmed by what she'd found. The company's distribution center was its central hub for all Fazbear-related toys, costumes, and decor. It shipped to restaurants and specialty and retail stores. She'd looked at some of those toys and costumes, and they were unsettling to say the least. What better container for pure malevolence than some creepy toy? Nurse Ackerman suspected that whatever was inside the man in room 1280 had a plan. A plan that needed to be stopped.

Checking over her shoulder one more time, Nurse Ackerman picked up her pace. She hoped she'd have enough time to finish the job at hand before Nurse Fremont finished her lunch.

Nurse Fremont was the other challenge the nurses had to handle. The timing of her addition to the hospice wing roster was unfortunate. She was just a little too perky, a little too energetic for comfort. Nurse Ackerman had given Nurse Fremont a little test on her first day, talking about the man in room 1280 and Father Blythe in the break room while Nurse Fremont ate. If she'd turned and asked what they were talking about, they'd have included her. But she'd just eavesdropped, and Nurse Ackerman didn't trust eavesdroppers.

At the doorway to room 1280, Nurse Ackerman paused. She looked behind her. The hallway was empty. It was time.

Putting her shoulders back, Nurse Ackerman entered the room. She even considered closing the door, but she couldn't do it. None of the nurses had ever closed themselves inside room 1280. Quite frankly, they were afraid to.

She only needed a minute anyway.

Crossing to the loathsome thing in the bed, Nurse Ackerman took out her first glass vial of morphine and thrust it onto the needle end of her syringe. She ignored the flutters of excitement that danced over her skin. It wasn't that she was eager to kill. It was just that it would be such a relief to rid her hospice wing, her hospital, her *world* of this stain upon mankind.

With a steady hand, Nurse Ackerman injected the first

of the morphine into the man's IV port. She watched the heart monitor. Its rhythm didn't falter.

She had suspected this would happen. Smoothly, she pulled out the second vial.

That's when she heard the giggle.

Nurse Ackerman pivoted toward the door, but no one was there.

Stepping away from the bed, she went to the door and looked out into the hallway. Had Nurse Fremont finished her lunch?

The hallway was empty.

Then Nurse Ackerman heard another giggle, and this time it was behind her.

A blast of cold rushed down her spine and tightened into a vice grip in her bowels. Slowly, as if about to face a wild animal she didn't want to spook, Nurse Ackerman turned.

She didn't know what she expected to see. She was prepared for literally anything. How could she not be? Anyone who had the man in room 1280 as a patient would have to be ready for anything.

But she saw nothing.

Everything was just as it had been when she entered the room.

Even so, she stood next to the man for several moments to be sure, watching him to see if she could discern a change. She couldn't.

Well, that wasn't true. She did notice one change.

The smell in the room was worse now than it had been when she first came in. It had intensified, as if someone had been fiddling with the hospital's thermostat, and had allowed the room to heat significantly. The odor was ghastly.

She'd better get on with it.

Nurse Ackerman still held the second vial of morphine, so she quickly inserted her syringe and emptied it into the IV port. Again, she watched.

And again, nothing.

Nurse Ackerman straightened her spine and pulled the rest of the morphine vials from her pocket. Eleven more. She laid them on the edge of the bed, in a tidy row. She'd inject them all if she had to, one right after the other. She wasn't going to wait for a result.

Reaching for the third vial, she heard the giggle again. Her hand stopped in midair.

The giggle came from *right next to her.*

A little black-haired boy stood by her side, looking up. He was grinning a grin so feral that it acted like a siphon, extracting the strength from Nurse Ackerman's limbs. She felt herself start to crumple toward the floor, and she caught herself on the edge of the bed just in time.

He was just a little boy. Why was she so afraid?

He ran out of the room, and Nurse Ackerman tried to steady her racing heart rate. She needed to get herself under control so she could return to what she needed to do.

But her mind, her memories, wouldn't let her find calm. Instead, she was transported, wholly against her will, into her past. She was deposited next to the bed of her dying son, the one who had left this world and had taken with him every smile Nurse Ackerman might ever have smiled. Feeling the agony as if she was living it, Nurse Ackerman experienced for the millionth time that moment when her son's death had reached into her heart and had torn it apart.

She hadn't always been this shell of a woman. But Elijah's death had carved her out, leaving a barely functioning person to find a place among living beings who tortured her with reminders of the life she'd once shared with her son. Even though her heart was frozen, she'd become a hospice nurse to help others who had to walk in her shoes.

Stop this right now! she admonished herself. She didn't have time for this misery.

Nurse Ackerman pushed aside her past, along with the question of who the little boy was and why he was here. She also boxed up the puzzle of why he was so terrifying. One thing at a time, she told herself.

Once again, she reached for a vial. Before her fingers could close around it, though, a child-size shadow flashed in front of her.

As it streaked by, all the vials flew off the bed and hurtled toward the floor, where they shattered on impact.

Morphine puddled innocuously on the tiles.

Nurse Thomas's plan was simple because Nurse Thomas was simple.

A lover of growing flowers, cooking her family large fattening dinners, and needlepointing Bible verses, Nurse Thomas—Beatrice to her friends—had become a nurse because she also loved people, simply loved them. She wanted to serve them, however she could.

These truths about Nurse Thomas were a little counter to where she currently was and what she was currently doing. Right now, she stood outside room 1280 holding a pillow that she intended to use as a weapon.

But really, Nurse Thomas's goals were all congruent, she told herself. What she was about to do was an act of love, an act of love as pure and simple as she was. Beatrice was doing this for the same reason she did everything every day. She was doing it to help people.

Nurse Thomas looked over her shoulder. She was alone.

Just because she was doing this to help didn't mean she wanted to be seen doing it. No one besides Nurse Ackerman and Nurse Colton seemed to understand.

Pausing to say a short prayer outside of room 1280, Nurse Thomas hugged the pillow and then opened the door. She ducked her head as soon as she was in the room. She always did this in room 1280. It was a way of seeing well enough to do what she needed to do without having to look too closely at what was in the bed.

She didn't want to look at what was in the bed because it was the most grotesque thing she'd ever seen. A macabre conglomeration of writhing slime and fire-branded dross, the man-shaped mass of bone and tissue in the bed literally made Nurse Thomas's eyes burn, as if she was looking at a solar eclipse without shades. This effect was so intense that she'd even tried wearing sunglasses in this room to see if they'd help—which they didn't.

Breathing through her mouth because Nurse Ackerman was right—the smell was much worse than ever—Nurse Thomas approached the head of the bed. Giving the pillow one last squeeze, she held it in two hands, out in front of her.

She knew that Nurse Ackerman and Nurse Colton both thought her idea for killing the thing in this bed was silly. Maybe it was. But sometimes the easiest solution was the best one.

Morphine hadn't worked. That was for sure.

Nurse Thomas and her fellow nurses had spent an hour the night before discussing the little boy Nurse Ackerman had seen. Both Nurse Thomas and Nurse Colton had seen him, too. They even got Nurse Fremont to admit that she'd spotted him. Nurse Thomas didn't think Nurse Fremont had told them everything about what she'd seen, but she'd told them enough.

Earlier today, Nurse Thomas had overheard a couple orderlies talking about how people were seeing a little black-haired boy all over the hospital. The mystery of the boy wasn't necessarily related to room 1280.

Or was it?

After Nurse Fremont went home, and after handing over the hospice wing to the swing shift, the three nurses had shared coffee in the cafeteria and discussed the question that was even more important than the boy.

"What do you think the shadow was?" Nurse Thomas had asked Nurse Ackerman as she tried to ignore all the food smells in the room. She was hungry and couldn't wait to get home to cook macaroni and cheese and green bean casserole.

"I think it was *it* . . . whatever's inside that man."

"How did it get out?" Nurse Thomas asked.

"I can't explain any part of this!" Nurse Ackerman's voice was so loud it startled several nurses and doctors sitting nearby. Forks clattered. Someone dropped a glass. She immediately dropped her voice to a whisper. "It doesn't matter. What matters is we need to try again."

That's when Nurse Thomas volunteered her homespun little plan: she'd smother the man in room 1280 with a pillow.

Nurse Ackerman had wanted to try again with morphine, but Nurse Thomas convinced her that the man in room 1280, or whatever was inside the man in room 1280, would be ready for that. They needed to take him, or it, by surprise.

So here she was.

The previous night, Nurse Thomas had practiced. She'd done a bit of research, and she'd discovered it took about three minutes to suffocate someone with a pillow. She had to find out if she could hold a pillow forcefully over something for that long—or even longer. Learning from

Nurse Ackerman's experience, Nurse Thomas figured that if normally lethal doses of morphine didn't kill the thing, suffocation would take extra effort as well.

Nurse Thomas looked pillowy herself, but she wasn't. Hours of cooking, cleaning, gardening, and needlework had given her unexpected upper body strength. The strength came in handy when she did her pillow experiment on a doll she'd bought for a niece. She had no problem holding a pillow over the doll for seven minutes . . . although her muscles were burning a little by the time she was done.

She'd receive the strength she needed now, she was sure.

Nurse Thomas took a step toward the bed. She paused and listened, but there was no giggling of the kind Nurse Ackerman had described. Apparently the boy wasn't around.

Tightening her grip on the pillow, Nurse Thomas marched to the bed and shoved it down hard over the man's face, or at least over where his face should have been. Nurse Thomas's muscles were tensed, poised, and ready for anything.

Yet nothing happened . . . at first.

Then the pillow started filling with blood. It came through the middle of the pillow, and soon began spreading outward, seeping inexorably toward Nurse Thomas's fingers. But she didn't let go. She was focused on the end result.

After six and a half minutes, the monitor's steady

beep . . . beep . . . beep picked up its pace. Then, glory be, after another minute it shifted to the sustained tone of a flatline.

She was doing it!

Just a few more seconds should be enough.

The pillow was almost fully saturated with blood, and now Nurse Thomas noticed a sickly green fluid was coming through the pillow as well. She gagged but kept pressing.

That's when a shadow darted in front of Nurse Thomas and tore the pillow from her grasp. Before she could even think about trying to retrieve it, the pillow ruptured, its contents ejecting into the room . . . and all over her.

Sticky, odious blood went into her mouth and up her nose. Putrid slime flew into her eyes. And bits of cloth and foam stuck to the fluids that sluiced over her skin and coagulated in her hair.

Nurse Thomas didn't make a sound, but the monitors did. They shifted from a steady flatline tone back to a stable, even rhythm.

Nurse Thomas fainted into the middle of the sickening mess on the floor.

Arthur was getting frustrated. He didn't often get frustrated because he believed in universal timing. But that timing seemed to be a little off right now.

It was now five days since the man in room 1280 had been able to communicate with him. Since then, Arthur had been back to see the man daily, although he'd only stayed a couple hours each time. The rest of the time he was at the hospital, he was in the administration offices trying to get someone to listen to him.

"What harm could it do?" he'd said over and over, to at least a dozen different people.

He simply couldn't understand why moving the man in room 1280 was such a bad thing. Either he'd survive the experience and get whatever it was he wanted from his visit to Fazbear Entertainment Distribution Center, or he wouldn't. And if he didn't, well, Arthur couldn't help but think that would be a mercy.

The hospital administration didn't agree.

They also were distracted. It seemed that the whole hospital was abuzz about repeated sightings of a little dark-haired boy wearing an alligator mask. Dozens of people had seen the boy, but thus far, no one had been able to talk to him.

The police had been called in to find the boy and figure out where he belonged, but none of the officers ever spotted him. Every time the boy was seen, and officers rushed to the location reported, the boy was gone before the officers arrived. Meanwhile, patients and staff had seen the boy in locations all over the hospital. Apparently, a janitor even saw him in the hospital's basement, near the backup generators. As far as the hospital administration and the police could determine, no one was missing a child who matched his description.

Because no one had spoken with the boy and no one had been able to grab him, people now were wondering whether he was a ghost. A ghost in an alligator mask—of all things.

But that wasn't Arthur's business. He had his own problems to solve.

And today he was taking a breather from arguing with hospital personnel: he was having lunch with Mia.

"Here I am," Mia called out as she wove her way through the wooden picnic tables in the outdoor eating area off the cafeteria.

The tables were set up on pinkish stone pavers, within a larger patio lined with stone planters filled with orange and yellow mums. A half dozen dark-eyed juncos and a couple sparrows hopped among the flowers.

The sun had reasserted its dominance over the sky, and it was lighting up all of fall's jewel colors, turning the trees surrounding Heracles Hospital into masterpieces of brilliant reds, yellows, and oranges. Only the faintest of breezes made the tree branches sway and the leaves on the ground gambol about. It was a glorious day.

Mia's bright presence made it even better.

"I hope you haven't been waiting long," Mia said.

"Not at all." Truthfully, Arthur had been here for twenty-five minutes. But she was only fifteen minutes late.

"I also hope you didn't bring your lunch, because my boyfriend made these amazing provolone and corned beef sandwiches. Oh, you're not a vegetarian are you? Or can you eat corned beef? Is it kosher or whatever?"

Arthur smiled. "I'm not a vegetarian," he said.

"Oh good," Mia replied. She pulled out two thick sandwiches on hoagie rolls, both tightly wrapped in plastic, and handed one to him.

"So how's it going with admin?" she asked as soon as she'd taken a bite and washed it down with a soda.

"It's not," admitted Arthur.

Taking the fact that he'd run into Mia every day he'd been at the hospital as a sign of encouragement, Arthur had finally told her he was trying to get permission to take a patient out of the hospital to a place the patient had requested to visit.

Mia had surprised Arthur when she responded, "Oh, the man in room 1280?"

"How did you know?" he asked.

"I overheard Nurse Ackerman and the others talking about him, and they caught me listening, so they told me about him. I haven't seen him yet or anything. They say I'm not ready for that. I think I'm more ready than they think I am, but whatever. I'm plenty busy." She took a bite of sandwich.

"I'm not sure you're ready, either," Arthur said. He hated the idea of this cheerful girl having to see . . . But wait, that wasn't very kind, was it? The man couldn't help what he looked like.

Arthur bit into his sandwich and immediately knew why Mia was so crazy about her boyfriend. The man was a sandwich saint. "This is amazing," he said.

"I know. Right?" She grinned.

They both chewed for a few seconds. When Mia finished chewing, she said, "The man in room 1280's that bad, huh?"

Arthur shrugged.

"I've overheard them talking about other things, too," Mia said.

"Who?" he asked.

"Nurse Ackerman and the others."

Mia was quiet for a minute, so Arthur prompted her. "What other things?" he asked.

Mia bit her lower lip. Then she waved a hand. "It doesn't matter." She took a drink of soda. "You've heard about the boy, right?"

Arthur laughed. "How could I not? Everyone's talking about him."

"I saw him," Mia said. Was she bragging?

"Really?"

"At least four times so far. Always wearing that silly mask."

Arthur settled in with his sandwich and listened to Mia describe the curly-haired boy with the devilish grin. He had to admit mild curiosity about the child. Arthur himself hadn't seen him, but that was okay.

"You know," Mia said. "You could use the boy to your advantage."

"How?"

Arthur wasn't a fan of using anyone, much less a little

boy, but he figured he might as well hear what Mia had to say. He found her voice to be as comforting as one of Peggy's hot toddies on a cold night.

"Well, the whole thing is causing a mass of paperwork for the people in admin. It's a nightmare to document all the sightings and coordinate with the police, I'm sure. Why don't you suggest you're going to follow them around and bug the heck out of them unless they let you take the man to where he wants to go? I used to do that when I was a kid. If you just keep asking, keep pestering people when they're really busy, they eventually say yes just to get rid of you. Works like a charm." She laughed and bit into her sandwich.

Arthur thought about it for a second. "That's not a bad idea."

Mia grinned. She had a piece of lettuce caught between her two front teeth. On her, it was charming.

Nurse Colton had a plan she was sure was better than those of Nurse Ackerman and Nurse Thomas. It had the advantage of being both simple and sophisticated. And it should also be lethal, she expected, assuming she wasn't thwarted by the mysterious shadow that had derailed the actions of her fellow conspirators.

But unlike Nurse Ackerman and Nurse Thomas, Nurse Colton expected the shadow to intervene. She had a plan to stop it.

Nurse Thomas had been home sick for two days.

Neither Nurse Ackerman nor Nurse Colton knew whether the sickness was physical or psychological. Obviously, anyone who'd experienced a monstrous deluge of foul bodily fluids like those that had drenched Nurse Thomas had a right to get a little hysterical. Fainting seemed an appropriate reaction. Nurse Colton didn't begrudge Nurse Thomas at all for just escaping consciousness for a while.

Nurse Colton and Nurse Ackerman had both been masked, gowned, and gloved when they'd cleaned up the detonated pillow. They'd also put camphor on their upper lips to dampen the smells. However, they'd both gagged repeatedly for the hour it took to clean the room . . . and Nurse Thomas.

What was the shadow?

That was the discussion the three women had at Nurse Thomas's house the previous evening. They'd decided it was an extension of the thing in the bed . . . or what was inside the thing in the bed.

This was why Nurse Colton thought she knew what to do about it. She had some experience with this sort of thing, and she felt pretty good about her plan.

Whereas Nurse Ackerman was cut off from her emotions and Nurse Thomas was too enslaved to hers, Nurse Colton thought she was the perfect balance of heart and brain. She felt and felt deeply, yes, but she also had a depth of reason that the other two women lacked. She had to have this balance. Nurse Colton had been on her own since she was sixteen.

When her parents died, Nurse Colton had decided to forego foster care. She'd instead run away, found a woman who made fake IDs, and gotten a job on a cruise ship, a job that came with free room and board. Over time, she'd saved up enough money to pay for nursing school. Now she was here because people like her lost people like her parents. It was only right to use what she knew about it to help others.

On her way down the hall to room 1280, Nurse Colton saw the little boy run into the storage room. She still had no idea whether he was real or supernatural. She suspected the latter, but if he was some kind of ghost, she didn't know what to make of him, and she didn't know how to make him go away. So she figured she'd deal with one mystery at a time.

At the door of room 1280, Nurse Colton stopped and set down the tote bag she carried. Looking back down the hall, she pulled out eucalyptus oil combined with a carrier oil. She put a dab of the oil mixture above her upper lip. The strong aroma, she hoped, would block out the contemptible stink in the room.

After one more look down the hall, Nurse Colton pulled a plain white pillar candle out of her tote. She stepped into room 1280, and she set down the candle. Then she pulled out another candle, and set it a couple feet from the first one. One after the other, she placed candles around the perimeter of the space. Once she had the candles in place, Nurse Colton pulled a lighter from her tote bag, and she methodically lit every candle.

After the candles were lit, Nurse Colton closed her eyes and imagined expanding the candles' light until it filled the entire room. Then she turned and looked at the man in the bed, and she said, "This room is filled with the light of good. No shadow can enter or do mischief here."

She stood very still to be sure her intention was strong enough. Yes, it felt right.

Nurse Colton believed in the power of intention and human will. Both had helped her survive the loss of her parents and build a life on her own terms. Both would serve her now, she was sure of it.

Good. It was time.

Nurse Colton set down her tote bag and looked at the man in the bed. Unlike Nurse Thomas, Nurse Colton preferred to face the ugliness of life head-on. Yes, the man's fire-blighted bones and nearly calcified insides filled her with revulsion, but she could handle it.

Now she was going to rid the world of it.

Nurse Colton pulled out a syringe. It held no drug. It was a syringe of air. She figured if the thing in the bed could breathe, it could die of an air embolism.

Leaning forward, Nurse Colton began injecting the air into the IV port in the thing's forearm. She had no doubt she'd succeed because she knew she was standing in a protective circle. This circle was so strong that even if the shadow—whatever it was—was inside the circle when she cast it, the circle would stop the shadow from doing what it wanted to do.

As she began to depress the plunger on the syringe . . . her protection circle failed.

Lacerating the air in front of Nurse Colton, a shadow swept across the syringe. The syringe leaped from her hand, spinning just once before shooting like an arrow toward Nurse Colton's throat. Stabbing deep into her skin just above the collarbone, it vibrated, sending jitters through her neck.

Nurse Colton knew if she didn't grab the syringe immediately, the air in that syringe was going to kill her. So she reacted instantly, jerking the syringe from her neck only to have it snatched from her again. This time, she held up her hands in surrender.

The syringe fell to the floor and snapped in half. Then a hot, musty blast of air rushed through the room and extinguished every candle flame. The candles flew back and smacked the walls.

Nurse Colton had never had her intention so violently defied, and she was rattled. But she wasn't going to show it.

She looked at the vile mass on the bed. "We'll find a way," she said.

A giggle came from outside the hallway.

Nurse Colton rushed to the door and she ran right into Nurse Fremont, who stood like a statue, staring down the hall.

"He went that way," Mia told Nurse Colton.

"Who?" she asked, looking stunned.

"The little boy."

"I'm beginning to think it's not a little boy," Nurse Colton admitted.

Mia nodded. "Me too."

The nurses stood in silence, looking down the hall. Then Mia asked, "What just happened?"

"You saw?"

Mia nodded. She wasn't afraid.

Nurse Colton cocked her head and studied Mia for several moments. "You're curious," she concluded correctly.

Mia nodded again.

"Okay. Come in." Nurse Colton went back into room 1280.

Mia tried to follow, but she had to stop in the doorway and cover her nose.

Mia liked to keep lists. She kept lists of the best things in life—best experiences, best sights, best tastes, best smells, best sounds, etc. And she kept lists of the worst things in life. Three of the smells on her worst smells list were rotten eggs, dead bodies (she'd unfortunately once been the one to discover the body of an elderly woman in an adjacent apartment without family to check on her . . . it was the smell that had led to the discovery), and a skunk's spray.

The smell in this room was worse than Mia's three worst smells combined.

"Oh," she said.

"Try this." Nurse Colton handed Mia a small container of essential oil. Mia sniffed it and then rubbed some of it above her upper lip.

It was better but not great. Still, Mia stepped into the room.

She didn't know what she'd expected to see but it wasn't this. What *was* this?

"The poor, poor man," she whispered.

Nurse Colton looked at the bed and sighed. Then she said, "Yes. But the man isn't the problem."

Mia glanced at Nurse Colton and then returned her gaze to what lay in the bed.

Mia had never been squeamish. In fact, she kind of enjoyed the gory stuff. She'd looked at the elderly cadaver she'd discovered, stared right at the mass of maggots and thought, *Cool.* It was nature at work.

But this?

This wasn't nature.

This was the exact opposite of nature. It was a violation of the very idea of nature.

Neither a skeleton nor a man, this brittle bone container of decaying organs and tissue still somehow managed to sustain enough life to result in the brain activity Mia could see on one of the monitors. That was just wrong, fundamentally wrong.

"It's what's inside that's the problem," Mia said.

"Yes," Nurse Colton said.

Mia thought about the conversations she'd heard. The

conversations about evil and extermination. Now they had context.

Turning, Mia met Nurse Colton's direct gaze and nodded. "I think I understand."

Mia was a genius.

Arthur had felt like a spoiled child, following the administration staff around, asking over and over for permission to take the man in room 1280 to Fazbear Entertainment Distribution Center. He couldn't, however, argue with the results.

In spite of the vociferous and numerous objections voiced by the nurses on the hospice wing and even from others in the hospital (when they signed a petition), Arthur received a call late the evening before telling him he could take the man in room 1280 to Fazbear Entertainment Distribution Center *if* he came in and signed a multitude of papers absolving the hospital from any responsibility for whatever might result from the trip.

So, once again, Arthur pedaled toward Heracles Hospital. Today, he was wearing full rain gear because there was no arguing with the colossal churning storm clouds that dominated the sky. Not a single ray of the sun's light was finding its way through the black and gray cloud stacks that made it seem more like twilight than 10:10 in the morning.

Rain began falling as the hospital came into view. Arthur kept his head down, navigating by the markings for the bicycle lane at the right edge of the driveway. Every car that sped past sprayed Arthur with water and buffeted Ruby so her tires wobbled a little on the pavement. Arthur was relieved when he glanced up and saw he was almost to the portico.

But then his feet fumbled with Ruby's pedals. Had he just seen what he thought he'd seen?

Glancing up at the portico, taking in the majesty of the building's vine-covered facade and its intricate statuary, he was sure he'd just seen a child's head peek out from behind the stone Cerberus.

Arthur braked, wiped his eyes, and stared through the gauzy rain curtains separating him from the hospital. He squinted, focusing as intensely as he could on Cerberus and the top of the columns flanking the portico. No. Nothing was there.

He must have imagined what he'd seen. All that talk about the little boy; it had put the idea in his mind.

But . . . he didn't think he'd imagined it.

Arthur tried to take a last look, but the rain curtains turned into solid walls of water pounding the earth as if Mother Nature was trying to obliterate an enemy. Now Arthur could see nothing but rain, so he stood on Ruby's pedals and got both himself and his poor drowned bicycle under cover.

Ten minutes later, still dripping water wherever he went because he carried his wet rain gear with him, Arthur sat in front of a very different desk from all the desks he'd sat in front of during his campaign for the trip to Fazbear Entertainment Distribution Center. This wasn't the desk of some low-level paper-pusher. This was the desk of someone with power—in this case, legal power. Arthur sat in front of the desk of Carolyn Benning Graves, Heracles Hospital's head attorney.

Ms. Graves had much nicer chairs than Pete and all the others in the administration office. Arthur was quite comfortable in a burgundy leather wingback chair.

"You understand, Father Blythe, that any damages resulting from this patient transport, be they property or personal, shall be wholly and completely your responsibility?"

Arthur nodded. "I understand." His stomach did a somersault. What if something went wrong?

Arthur adjusted his attitude. Where was his faith? He and the man in room 1280 would be watched over.

The attorney pushed a stack of papers across the clean polished surface of her mahogany desk. "Please read through these agreements, sign where indicated, and initial where specified."

Arthur started to lean forward.

"Not here, Father Blythe," Ms. Graves said. She made a motion, and a thin, well-dressed young woman appeared and picked up the papers. "Please go with Ms. Weber here. She'll take you to a place where you can read and sign. I'm afraid I have another appointment."

Arthur dutifully vacated the wingback chair, feeling victorious.

★ ★ ★

Mia hovered in the hallway outside the hospital's legal offices. She'd been told Father Blythe was still signing papers giving him the authority to take the man in room 1280 to Fazbear Entertainment Distribution Center. In spite of those papers, she hoped she'd be able to talk him into giving up the idea.

Leaning against the wall, Mia nodded and smiled at everyone who went by, but she didn't really *see* anyone. Her mind wasn't in this hallway with her. It was reviewing what had led her to this place and this time and this mission.

Mia hadn't really understood why the only job she could find was on the hospice wing at Heracles Hospital. She was highly qualified and had excellent references. She should have been able to get a better position. In fact, she'd been feeling pretty resentful that she was stuck with what she'd gotten.

If it wasn't for her boyfriend continually reminding her that the job was a stepping stone, she'd have been pretty miserable. But between his encouragement, his wonderful sandwiches, and her own naturally optimistic nature, she'd been reasonably content here . . . except for being creeped out by her fellow nurses on the hospice wing and their disturbing hushed conversations.

But now she understood them. Oh boy, did she ever!

Mia also understood why she had gotten this job. She was needed here.

"Why hello, Mia."

Mia focused and realized Father Blythe was standing in front of her.

"What are you doing here?"

Mia smiled as she watched Father Blythe juggle a stack of papers, orange rain gear, and his bright red bicycle helmet. The rain gear dripped on Father Blythe's black leather shoes. For some reason, he always smelled like coconuts.

"Actually, I'm here to talk to you, Father," Mia said. She glanced around the busy hallway, then she looked down the hall to a small waiting area. "Could you come with me a second?"

Father Blythe glanced at his watch. "Peggy's going to be meeting me out front with the church van. It's wheelchair accessible. I'm going to trade her Ruby for the van." Then he looked into Mia's eyes. "But okay."

Mia took Father Blythe's arm and led him down the hall. She smiled at everyone as they went, noticing that several nurses gave Father Blythe disapproving frowns.

In the waiting area, Mia sat in one of the tan plush chairs and motioned to the one next to it. Father Blythe sat beside her.

"What is it, Mia? You seem troubled."

"I am."

She looked at Father Blythe's warm brown eyes. He had such a kind face, such an open face. She could see that he'd known suffering, but she could also tell that he was resolute in his intention to see the good in everything. He had one of those mouths that curved upward, even when his face was expressionless. He was designed for seeing light in darkness.

Realizing that he was waiting for her to speak, Mia looked around to be sure they were alone. She leaned as close to Father Blythe as she could without being weird, inhaled, and then said in a rush, "Father, I know I gave you that advice about how to get permission to take the man in room 1280 out of the hospital. But you can't take him. You just can't. The man in room 1280 . . . he can't leave this place. I can't explain why I know this, but I know it. He can't go where he wants to go. You can't take him. The other nurses are right. I thought they were lunatics. I admit it. I did. But now I understand. They're right. There's something in that poor man. There's something in there, and you can't take it where it wants to go. You can't. It will be devastating, even catastrophic, if you do. I don't know how or why but I do know it. You have to believe me. I—" Mia stopped. She realized that she could gush forth another thousand or even million words and Father Blythe wasn't going to change his mind. It was right there on his face.

Lips pressed into compassionate regret, thick gray brows drawn together, crinkles drawn in at the corner of his wide-set eyes, slightly weak chin tucked—these were all telegraphing what was going to come out of Father Blythe's mouth.

"Mia," he said when she'd finished her case, "I'm so sorry. But I have to take this man where he wants to go. It's his last request."

"Just because it's his last request doesn't make it a good one," Mia attempted futilely.

"Why is this so important to you?" Father Blythe asked.

Mia had no logical answer. She wasn't about to explain what she'd seen in his hospital room; she knew how crazy it sounded, and she couldn't lose this job. But beyond what she'd seen, all she had was a feeling, an intuition. Maybe it was a premonition. "It just is," she said finally.

Father Blythe set down his rain gear and bicycle helmet. He tucked the papers under his arm, and he took Mia's hand.

"Mia, I've lived long enough to see the kind of evil that exists in our world. I haven't seen it all, by any means, but I've seen more than enough to understand that my glass-is-always-full attitude has no basis in earthly reality. I should be jaded by now, I suppose. I should be pessimistic, ready to see the worst. But I'm not. I'm not because I choose not to let the past color the way I see the present. I choose to expect, in every moment, to find what's good."

"But what if you don't?"

"Then there's always the next moment."

"And what if there isn't?" Mia could hear the fear in her voice. She brushed away the tears that threatened to spill.

Father Blythe breathed in and out slowly. "Then I'll move on to whatever my journey holds next for me, I suppose. That's all we can do. That's all I'm trying to do for the man in room 1280."

Mia swallowed and nodded. "You won't change your mind."

"I'm sorry, but no."

Mia stood, and Father Blythe gathered his things.

"May I hug you, Father?" she asked.

"Of course."

They hugged, and she tried to pour into Father Blythe the inexplicably huge amount of warmth she felt for him. Or was it worry?

They separated, and he said, "Bye, Mia. I'll see you again soon."

"Bye, Father," she said as he gave her a little wave and headed down the hall.

Fazbear Entertainment Distribution Center was a massive collection of reddish and whitish buildings that Arthur couldn't believe he had never noticed before. Looking like long flat metal-sided blocks haphazardly placed in clusters by a gargantuan child, the buildings must have been here at least twenty years. Low slung and dotted with narrow windows, every one of them needed paint or at least a good cleaning. (Arthur was pretty sure the buildings had been bright white and bright red when they'd first been built.) Along the sides of most of the buildings, slanted drives led to cracked concrete loading docks. Even the big rig trailers tucked into at least a dozen of those docks looked like they'd been in service for a good long while. Some were rusted. Many were dented. All were dirty.

Admittedly, it was a dreary day, but Arthur was sure that even in bright sunlight, this distribution center would look like it needed a lot of TLC.

The address of the distribution center, which Peggy had gotten for Arthur along with instructions for getting there, turned out not to be a building but rather a small empty guard house and an open gate. Once through this abandoned entry, Arthur didn't know exactly what to do. He realized now that the man's designation of the Fazbear center was almost like picking "Iowa" as the place he wanted to visit. What specific part of this place did the man want to go to?

Arthur glanced in the rearview mirror at the sheet-enshrouded bundle in the wheelchair, locked into place behind the van's passenger seat. He still wasn't used to seeing the palpitating dried organs and veins in an upright position. He also wasn't used to the smell.

Although he'd tried to talk himself out of it for the trip from Heracles Hospital to Fazbear Entertainment, Arthur was sure the man smelled worse with every mile they traveled. The van was filled with a grim stench of sulfur, feces, decomposition, blood, and bile.

Ever since the man in room 1280 had been transferred from his bed to the wheelchair, he'd been leaking blood and viscous black fluids. The treacly mixtures were now soaking the sheet around the man and pooling on the van floor. Arthur knew it was going to take hours to clean up the van after this trip.

In spite of this, the man sat upright in his seat. He was strapped in, but his head wasn't drooping. Of course he had no eyes, but his eye sockets were directed ahead, as if he could see exactly where they were.

Feeling less and less sure about what he was doing, Arthur told himself to stop judging the poor man based on his appearance. He cleared his throat. "So do you know where you want to go?"

Arthur didn't really expect a response, but he got one.

The man raised one of his crusty finger bones and pointed it in a direction that seemed to indicate the largest building in the Fazbear collection. It was also the building, Arthur noticed now, that had a large covered courtyard leading to a glass-fronted wall. That was probably the main entrance.

Arthur realized he should have called ahead to get permission to bring the man into the distribution center, but maybe his failure to do so had been unconscious. What was that old saying? It was better to ask for forgiveness than for permission? Something like that. Arthur didn't want another battle like the one he'd had to fight at the hospital.

To that end, Arthur decided not to head to the main entrance the man had indicated.

"I'm going to find a side entrance, I think," Arthur said out loud. "Something more private. Are you all right with that?"

The man didn't move, but Arthur thought he could

hear a sloppy percussion emanating from the man's chest. Was Arthur hearing the man's heartbeat? Arthur suppressed the shivers that started at the top of his head and did an arpeggio down his neck to his spine.

Arthur put the van in gear and pulled it around to the side of the main building. The van's tires made fizzing sounds on the wet pavement. Arthur wondered how he'd transport the man into the building without getting him wet. Somehow, dousing a body with barely there skin didn't seem like a good idea.

As soon as Arthur turned the corner of the big building, he saw the solution to his problem. This side of the building had van-size loading docks under an overhang.

"Ask and ye shall receive," Arthur said, smiling. He said a prayer of thanks for the help.

At the far end of this row of loading docks, a couple of husky workers wearing back braces and scowls loaded boxes into a dirty white van. They paid no attention when Arthur pulled the church van parallel to the platform at the opposite end of the docks.

"This should work," he said to the man. Of course he got no response.

Jumping out of the van, Arthur took in a cleansing lungful of fresh air. Well, not fresh exactly. The air smelled like grease and solvents, but at least it smelled better than the air in the van.

Arthur opened the side door, removed the wheelchair, and jockeyed it into position on the ramp. Trying not to be too prissy about it, Arthur touched the blood-stained sheet and adjusted it to better cover the man. He had nothing to wipe his fingers on, but he ignored the issue and wheeled the man into the building.

Inside the roll-up door openings of the loading docks, the building revealed itself to be the heart of the Fazbear Entertainment Distribution Center. Stretching so far into the distance that Arthur couldn't see the end of them, floor-to-ceiling shelves held stacks and stacks of boxes and plastic-enclosed packages. Peggy had told Arthur that Fazbear Entertainment created parts and costumes for animatronics used in restaurants and other venues. It also created costumes for humans to wear and various toys and other merchandise related to their most famous characters. Arthur assumed that's what was in all the boxes and packages. It also explained the faded murals on the pale yellow walls—the murals depicted a variety of outlandish animal characters of questionable purpose. Despite their cheery appearance, Arthur couldn't be sure they were intended to be friendly.

In front of the shelving area, a series of conveyors took boxes and packages on journeys through the building— journeys that would probably end up near loading docks. A few workers monitored the conveyors while others drove forklifts down the rows of the shelving area. A tall man with red hair wandered about, carrying a clipboard, but he wasn't looking this way.

The building was surprisingly quiet. Only the muted

clatter of the conveyor, the hum of the forklift motors, and a few shouts and thumps broke up the cavernous hush of the place.

"Well, here we are." Arthur turned to look at the man.

And then the man started to convulse.

Several thoughts tangled in Arthur's head as he watched the bones and organs and tissue in the wheelchair shake so uncontrollably that some of the man's rib bones cracked. When blood flew and tissue cinders began spewing, Arthur thought, *They should have let me bring a nurse* and *What should I do?* and *Why did I sign all those papers?* and *Please guide me.*

Arthur leaned over the wheelchair just as the man collapsed into a mound of bone and an indescribable mass of fried human parts. At a loss, Arthur began to pray silently.

But before Arthur could get through two words of his prayer, the man's remains heaved. Then they burst like a nightmarish egg blowing open to disgorge new life.

Expelling rank-smelling sticky black blood and a tar-like substance in a frightful spray all over Arthur and the building's smooth concrete floor, the explosion of bone and veins and organs happened in an instant. In that instant, Arthur saw a void in the remains gape like a portal to hell itself. Then he was frantically wiping nauseating fluids and slimy body bits from his face. As he did this, he saw the man's body tumble from the wheelchair, and Arthur knew the man was dead.

Instinctively, Arthur began praying again. But as he

prayed, he heard something that wiped even the thought of prayer from his mind.

He heard a rush of pattering footsteps, little sprightly footsteps capering away toward the shelving area of the building.

What was that?

Arthur wiped his eyes again and looked around. At first, all he saw was the man's remains. For the first time since Arthur had gathered the courage to look at the man, all the exposed insides were still.

Then Arthur's gaze landed on a trail of tiny footprints that were stamped in the man's charred blood and fluids. He followed the trail and saw the footprints continue away from the man, etching the floor in the man's blood like fearful hieroglyphs marking the way.

The way to where?

The man had moved on. But something hadn't.

"Father? Is everything okay?" A man's voice, pitched high in shock, asked Arthur.

Arthur turned.

The speaker was the redheaded man with the clipboard. He stared at the floor, his face blanched, his eyes wide.

"Actually, no, I don't think everything is okay," Arthur said. For the first time in his life, he was sure of it.

ABOUT THE AUTHORS

Scott Cawthon is the author of the bestselling video game series *Five Nights at Freddy's*, and while he is a game designer by trade, he is first and foremost a storyteller at heart. He is a graduate of The Art Institute of Houston and lives in Texas with his wife and four sons.

Andrea Rains Waggener is an author, novelist, ghost-writer, essayist, short story writer, screenwriter, copywriter, editor, poet, and a proud member of Kevin Anderson & Associates' team of writers. In a past she prefers not to remember much, she was a claims adjuster, JCPenney's catalogue order-taker (before computers!), appellate court clerk, legal writing instructor, and lawyer. Writing in genres that vary from her chick-lit novel, *Alternate Beauty*, to her dog how-to book, *Dog Parenting*, to her self-help book, *Healthy, Wealthy, & Wise*, to ghostwritten memoirs to ghostwritten YA, horror, mystery, and mainstream fiction projects, Andrea still manages to find time to watch the rain and obsess over her dog and her knitting, art, and music projects. She lives with her husband and said dog on the Washington coast, and if she isn't at home creating something, she can be found walking on the beach.

Elley Cooper writes fiction for young adults and adults. She has always loved horror and is grateful to Scott Cawthon for letting her spend time in his dark and twisted universe. Elley lives in Tennessee with her family and many spoiled pets and can often be found writing books with Kevin Anderson & Associates.

Larson sat at his desk ignoring everything else in the office. On any normal day, he'd have had trouble concentrating while Roberts sprayed air freshener toward Powell's desk, while Powell bellowed at Roberts for spraying Powell's garlic-heavy meatball sandwich, while two drunk bikers hauled in for fighting continued trying to assault each other, and while the rest of the people in the office either talked on the phone or to one another. But today wasn't a normal day. Today, a marching band could have been doing formations between the desks and Larson wouldn't have cared. Today, he was on to something. Or at least he thought he was.

Bending over the papers and photos in front of him, guarding them with his elbows so he didn't have to explain his ideas to anyone else, Larson first pored over the photos of the Phineas Taggart crime scene.

They showed exactly what he remembered seeing when he'd arrived at the factory-to-crazy-scientist-laboratory-conversion weeks before. Viewing the scene had been like looking at a modern-day Frankenstein's lab. The room where the scientist's remains had been found had been packed full of scanning equipment, modified in incomprehensible ways, and hooked up to the strangest collection of junk he'd ever seen. Much of the junk had been just as mystifying as the equipment modifications—gears and hinges and mannequin parts and antique contraptions that looked like medieval torture devices. But one collection of junk had been combined in an especially disturbing way. Looking at it had twisted Larson's insides and put his blood in a deep freeze.

Because he'd been so rattled by what he was looking at, he hadn't looked at it closely. Now, he realized, he'd been an idiot. He should have looked harder. If he had, he'd have figured out what the Stitchwraith was a lot faster.

Or would he have?

Even if he'd put it together, mightn't it have taken him some time to come to terms with it?

Although he was sure now, he wasn't *totally* sure because what he was sure of was totally insane. If he was truly certain, he'd be telling his colleagues. Instead, he was peering at the evidence as if it was a treasure he wasn't willing to share.

Larson looked at the junk conglomeration that had so horrified him. And he knew; he was looking at the beginnings of the strange figure he was looking for.

In the photo he held, the doll's head could be seen only

from the side. That's how Larson had seen it in Phineas's laboratory as well. This was why Larson hadn't immediately recognized the sketched face when he'd seen the picture in the chief's envelope. But that head—he was sure it was the head—was attached to a metal endoskeleton.

Okay, so the mysterious figure was always described as wearing a hooded cloak, but Larson remembered seeing a long and voluminous hooded trench coat in Phineas's clothing. That could easily have been misidentified as a cloak.

Larson set down the photo, and he began reading through the inventory list from Phineas's property. Running his finger down the list, he read the items aloud under his breath. He stopped at the tenth item down. There it was: one robotic dog, disassembled, manufactured by Fazbear Entertainment.

Larson looked at the endoskeleton again. It seemed to have an addition. So part of that dog could have been used on the endoskeleton.

Okay, so we have an animatronic endoskeleton linked to a part that came from a Fazbear Entertainment robotic dog. Was he making too much of a leap connecting the dots?

The dog connected to Fazbear Entertainment, which was connected to the Freddy's murders. And the dog connected to the thing with the sketched face. So that meant Larson's current investigation could be connected to the Freddy's murders.

A paper airplane hit the top of Larson's bent head. He slapped at it and frowned, looking up.

"Earth to Larson," Roberts said. The detective's close-set gray eyes were aimed at the photos Larson was shielding. "I asked what you were doing."

"Thinking."

"About what?"

"Stupid stuff, probably." No way was Larson going to tell his straight-arrow partner, wearer of tweed jackets with leather elbow patches and too-proud owner of a perfectly groomed goatee, about his fledgling theory.

"Want to grab some lunch?"

"No thanks."

Roberts stared at Larson for a moment. Larson stared back, his face as blank as he could make it.

"Okay," Roberts said.

Larson shot the paper plane back across his desk to Roberts. "Nice one," he said, hoping to distract Roberts from any suspicion that Larson was onto something. Roberts was almost as proud of his aerodynamic paper airplanes as he was of his facial hair.

Roberts grinned. "Thanks." He got up and strolled away from his desk.

Larson waited until Roberts was gone, and then stood. He needed to get over to the evidence locker. He'd chew on his theory on the way.

The old stone building had originally housed the city police department, but this was now the department's annex, where the more obscure functions of the police department were carried out and where all records and evidence were kept. In the evidence locker's musty basement aisles, Larson stood on a stepladder and pulled a stack of three battered boxes from a shelf above his head. Setting them on the floor, all three boxes side by side, Larson squatted in front of them and took off their lids.

He coughed when the persistent odor of smoke wafted up from the boxes. Then he peered into each box. Larson's heart rate was in onto-something mode, thumping loud and fast in his chest.

The fire, so far in the past it was almost ancient history in the department, had never been solved. Larson didn't know a lot about it, but he did know the fire was connected to one of the founders of Fazbear Entertainment. His idea was that if the Stitchwraith was connected to Fazbear Entertainment and was seen at the site of the fire, the Stitchwraith might have been looking for something that had been put into evidence years ago. He didn't think it was that much of a stretch to reach this conclusion.

But the first three boxes didn't do much to bolster his theory. He replaced their lids and climbed up the stepladder. He climbed back down, shifted the ladder, climbed back up again, and pulled another stack of boxes from the shelves. This time he took the lids off one at a time.

When he took the lid off the third box, he raised his eyebrows and nodded.

* ★ ★

Grim hadn't been back to the railroad yard since he'd seen the mysterious figure prying loose parts from the tracks. Something about that figure had done more than just make his teeth hurt. It had made him want to dig a very deep hole and crawl into it.

Since he didn't have a shovel or the strength to dig such a hole, Grim had decided instead to move his usual hangout place to the far end of town, where abandoned factories rubbed shoulders with several stalwart old neighborhoods and the west dock of the lake. He found a rusted but sturdy shed just outside of one of the abandoned factories, a factory that had been so recently vacated that a shabby forklift still squatted nearby.

The shed, although watertight and clean, hadn't been discovered by anyone else like Grim, so he set up house under a long, wide shelf below a dirty window. Because he knew others could be attracted to such deserted locales, he was happy that he found the shelf in his shed made a suitable lounging platform for keeping an eye on his surroundings.

And it was a good thing he kept an eye out, because on his third night in the shed, he spotted the mysterious figure. Happy that he was at least in his usual crazy thoughts tonight, he still had trouble continuing to breathe as he watched the figure drag a bag through a double-garage-door-size opening in the boxy metal factory shell.

What compelled him to follow the figure to see where it

went? Was it that curiosity he'd felt the last time he'd seen the figure or was it perhaps some self-destructive urge?

Maybe it was that crazy voice in his head.

Whatever it was, Grim found himself scurrying stealthily, and perhaps a bit unsteadily, toward the opening into which the figure disappeared. When he reached it, he hesitated for a second, questioning the wisdom of his actions, but he went through the opening anyway.

Preparing to be jumped the second he entered, Grim was surprised and relieved to find himself in an empty triple garage–size space that widened into another space beyond. And he was even more surprised and pleased to hear movement in that second space and see enough light to pick his way over the debris-strewn concrete floor.

The dragging movement he heard was disconcerting and would have sent any normal person running for his life. Grim, however, hadn't been normal for several years. When Grim reached the front edge of the second space, he paused. He waited, listening until the scrape and *shoosh* sound of the dragging bag was far enough away to make him feel fairly certain he could follow without running into his quarry.

It didn't take long for him to feel like he should make his move. Taking a deep breath for courage, he took another step. And he stopped.

He was in a huge square expanse, an expanse with flat walls and high ceilings, an expanse filled with piles of junk. He figured this was the main floor of the old factory. It was at least a couple thousand square feet in size, and its high ceiling peaked at a bank of skylights, which allowed murky daylight to brighten the area.

Grim realized he stood on an elevated rim of the floor, a rim about fifteen feet wide. It ran around the perimeter of the huge space. Several sets of concrete stairs with metal stair rails led down to a level about six feet lower. On that level, on one side of the cavernous square, a massive, dirty, blue trash compactor was set partway into the concrete floor. It had a filthy, scarred chute that led from the elevated rim down into its metal bowels. It was quiet and still now, but Grim could imagine it in action, pummeling trash and then tipping it out into a shallow concrete pit near the end of its lethal enclosure. Near the trash compactor chute, a small shelf hung on the wall. The shelf held a pot with two bright red flowers shaped like starfish. Grim couldn't imagine anything looking more out of place than those two flowers did next to the powerful eater of trash.

Grim blinked and watched the cloaked figure drag his bag to one of the junk piles. He couldn't see what was in the bag, but he glimpsed a doll's arm hanging from the opening. Dressed in a bright-blue dress with equally bright-pink ruffles, the arm looked so innocent and sweet. It didn't belong in this room of metal and mechanical junk. Nothing belonged in such a room. Because the junk in this room wasn't just any junk. It was the junk of nightmares, the junk of bloodcurdling histories. The junk in this room was a collection of the worst mechanical monstrosities imaginable. Spotting the remains he'd seen removed from the tracks, Grim also saw the carcass of a robotic dog and several partial animatronic characters. It looked like someone had blown up a factory of creepy robotic toys and then piled up their remains.

Not even the crazy voices in his head could convince Grim to stay in this room. He backed out and retreated as quietly and as fast as he could to his rusty shed.

Jake, aware that he was being watched but not concerned about it because he could sense the soul and the character of the person watching, emptied the latest bag of infected items on the shortest pile in the abandoned factory. It made him sad to see the doll's arm. Well, all of it made him sad, actually. Toys shouldn't have been things that held terror and anger and fear. They should have been containers for joy and love and laughter.

Ever since Andrew had told Jake about all the infected things, Jake had been using the thing he and Andrew were in to gather all the stuff Andrew had infected. When he first had the idea to do that, he wasn't sure how he'd actually *do* it. He didn't know what he and Andrew were in then, just that it was made of metal and it could move. But then he understood he was in an animatronic endoskeleton run by a battery pack. And he understood he was looking at the world through a doll's eyes. None of that felt strange to him. The only thing he thought was funny was that the thing they were in was wearing a hooded trench coat. Going around in a trench coat felt really silly.

And it was hard to go all over in this thing, too. Harder than he'd thought it would be. Andrew had infected so much stuff!

Jake hadn't understood how tiring it was going to be to use his will to get the locations from Andrew's mind *and* make the animatronic go all over the place finding the stuff. Jake was feeling so worn out, like he had before he'd left his little-boy body. He wasn't sure he could keep doing what he needed to do.

Maybe he should just give up and let go. Jake hadn't done anything wrong. Why did he have to be the one to fix Andrew's mess?

Wasn't he a good boy? Didn't he deserve to have some fun?

"I think we need peanuts, don't you, Jake?" a smiling man asked.

A crowd cheered and a different man called out, "Hot dogs! Get your hot dog here!"

"Maybe a hot dog too?" the smiling man said.

Jake froze with the empty bag in his hand.

Was that a memory? Did he just have a memory?

He cocked his head. Since he'd been in this metal endoskeleton, he hadn't had a sense of smell. But now he felt like he was inhaling the aromas of peanuts and hot dogs. He also could feel something new. His face . . . or the face of what he was in . . . suddenly felt warm, like he was outside in bright sunlight instead of where he was—inside, in a dingy factory.

This had to be a memory, because it for sure wasn't happening right now. It felt like a memory, and the man in his memory had said his name.

No, wait. It wasn't just a man. It was his dad. Jake had just experienced a memory of his dad!

"What are the flowers for?" Andrew asked.

Jake ignored him. He was concentrating. The memory, if that's what it was, had felt really good. Jake wanted more of it. He closed his eyes and focused on the smells and the sounds and the sensations.

"Let's have both," Jake's dad said. He motioned, and a man came over with a tray full of roasted peanuts in small bags.

Jake felt himself settle into his little-boy body. He looked out through the little boy's eyes, and he saw a big field of grass and a huge crowd of people.

"Jake? What about the flowers?" Andrew asked.

Jake didn't answer. Instead he picked up a watering can he'd left under the shelf holding the flowerpot. He walked over to water the flowers.

At the same time, he returned to his memory.

As Jake watched his dad exchange money for one of the bags from the tray, understanding came back to him. For the first time since he'd become aware of being in the animatronic he was in now, he fully knew himself as he truly was. He was Jake, the little boy, and he was reliving an afternoon at a baseball game with his dad. It felt so real, and . . .

Jake began to feel as if he was being sucked out of the

thing he was in. He felt like he was a puff of smoke, and he was being borne by an air current away from the being that had contained him. He could feel himself being pulled into the memory itself, and he intuitively understood that if he was enveloped in the memory, he could stay in that happy place forever.

The crack of a bat resounded, and the crowd rose to its feet, cheering.

"Get your glove up, Jake!" his dad shouted. Jake raised his baseball-gloved hand.

And he drifted even further from the animatronic he'd been in.

"Jake? Where are you going? Jake!" Andrew shouted.

Jake realized he could easily relax into this wonderful memory and allow the whole of who he was to be extracted from the animatronic that contained him and Andrew. He could stop trying so hard. He could go have fun.

"Jake!?" Andrew called out.

But Jake couldn't leave Andrew. His new friend had never known love, and if Jake left, Andrew would be lost forever. Jake couldn't let that happen.

Jake looked hard at the piles of trash in the compactor; he forced the memory from his mind. By putting his whole attention on what was here now, he wiped the memory away from his awareness like he was erasing a blackboard.

As he did, he settled back into his place in the animatronic. He watered the flowers, and he ignored Andrew's repeated questions.